BLUES IN THE DARK

BLUES IN THE DARK

A Nate Ross Novel

J.R. Sanders

For Rose, always the antidote to the blues.

Praise for Blues in the Dark

"Nate Ross, a PI with a rhythm and poetry all his own, navigating the City of Angels with clipped wings."—Craig Johnson, author of the Walt Longmire Series

"Ace Atkins fans should give this series a look."—*Publishers Weekly*

Chapter One

Count Basie's orchestra had been set to play the Palomar ballroom on Vermont, their first ever gig in L.A. I'd been looking forward to catching their show. I hadn't been to the Palomar since the summer of '35, when I was still a deputy sheriff. I'd been sitting in the audience the night Benny Goodman showed the town what swing music was. I liked the idea of visiting again to witness a little more music history. And there was nobody who could beat Basie.

Then, two days before the Count was due to play, there was a fire and the whole joint burned to rubble. Instead of seeing a historic show, I had to settle for being hired to look into the fire. The management claimed to have had some threats from a couple of their less savory competitors, and also from a few cranks who didn't like the idea of a black orchestra playing the revered joint. They suspected arson.

But before I'd done more than a little legwork, the fire department determined that the blaze was accidental. A bass player with Charlie Barnett's orchestra had let a rosin-coated rag fall across one of the hot footlights. I'd not only missed my shot at seeing more musical history made, but I lost a very sweet paying job. So it goes.

* * *

"You can't blame me, Nate. How was I supposed to know the big lummox was gonna trip over his feet?"

I'd hired Danny Isaac for a penny-ante job I took on for a sort of friend who owned a liquor store. A guy had taken to coming in every day, giving the shelves a thorough browse, but leaving without buying anything, and my client was convinced he wasn't leaving empty-handed.

Petty boosters weren't really in my line, but since I was friendly with the owner, I told him I'd see what I could do. I'd handed the job off to Danny for half the fifty dollars I was being paid.

Danny's protest roused Monte, who'd been lying peacefully on his blanket in the corner. Monte had terrified him ever since their first encounter. Danny had tried to give him a pat and learned that Monte took a little time to warm to strangers, was particular about who touched him, and had an intimidating way of making his feelings on the matter known. Of late, he'd started giving Danny a friendly greeting at the office door. Danny was convinced it was some sort of canine sucker play, but I knew it was just the big dog's devilish sense of humor.

I used Danny now and then because he was good at shadow work and could follow instructions, and because I liked the little goof. He wasn't the brightest, but he was more or less reliable. I could count on him not to stray too far out of legal bounds, but he was always good for a misdemeanor or two. He did irk me no end with his habit of asking dumb questions just to have something to say.

"You think I should have just shot him when he run?"

Case in point. "Over a bottle of booze? And why were you heeled—I told you no guns."

"It's a bad neighborhood."

"Anyway," I said, "If you were quicker, he couldn't have taken leg bail on you."

Danny had set himself up inside the store's dairy cooler, where he'd had a pretty good view of the better stock through the glass doors.

"I told you," he said, "My foot got stuck. I stepped in some spilled milk, and my shoe kind of got froze to the floor. Took me a second to bust it loose."

"Sure it did. Half asleep, more likely."

He looked wounded. "I was not. Anyhow, what's the guy sore about? I caught his thief, didn't I?"

"Yeah, but you busted an eight-dollar bottle of Scotch in the process."

"I say again—not my fault."

When Danny had tried to make the pinch, his bird saw him coming and took off like a deer. Danny chased him two blocks until the guy went over a board fence, got his feet tangled up when he hit the other side, and fell flat on his face. The bottle he'd shoved down the front of his pants smashed, and by the time the cops and ambulance arrived, he had damn near bled to death.

"Remember that line. You may have to try and convince a judge of that."

"You don't think the guy's gonna sue, do you?"

"I don't know Danny. The town's lousy with lawyers, and they've all got to eat."

Now he was looking worried. "Is he okay, at least?"

"He'll live, but he lost a nut."

He made a pained face. "Yeesh. You think he's still gonna be able to…you know…?" He punched a fist in the air.

"Maybe, but his kids will only grow three feet tall."

"For real?"

"Get out of here—I'm busy."

"How 'bout my twenty-five bucks?"

"You're joking, right?" He just stared at me until I took out my wallet. I counted out bills, resisted the urge to ball them up and pitch them at him. I tossed them on the desk instead. "There's seventeen. The broken bottle's on you."

"Aw, Nate…"

"Goodbye, Danny."

He stood up with a careful eye on Monte, picked up his money, and left without another word.

* * *

I get all kinds coming through the door in my trade. I get suspicious spouses looking to see if the mister or missus is playing hootchie-coo with another. Those I steer to my less particular competitors. That sort of job is messy, more dangerous than you'd think, and just try getting paid by a client after you've been the bearer of bad tidings accompanied by graphic 8 x 10 glossies. I get small business owners convinced that an employee is cooking the books or tapping the till. I get stolen property cases the cops don't have the time or inclination to spend shoe leather on. I even get the occasional lost dog or cat. What I don't get much is chauffeurs.

After Danny left, I whittled away most of the morning at a hated task: going over my books to make sure my billing was up to date, that I hadn't missed any expenses I should have billed clients for, and writing out a couple of discreet second notices—and one vaguely threatening third notice—to slow payers. Overall, if the fourth quarter of 1939 didn't far outpace the first three, retirement was not on the horizon for me.

Engrossed as I was in this depressing financial minutia, I didn't hear footsteps approaching my office. The door opened so softly it didn't even jangle the bell above the frame. My canine cohort, snoozing on his blanket as usual, gave no warning. If it hadn't been for a shift of light and shadow on the floor, I might not have even noticed.

I looked up to find a tall, slender bird standing just my side of the threshold. And *bird* was the word to describe him. He could have been thirty-five or seventy. He had a short body perched on top of long, broomstick-thin legs, and a large, nearly round head balanced on a scrawny neck. His long, narrow nose bent down at the tip. Wisps of dusty brown hair curled up from under his cap like feathers, and dark, heavy, unkempt brows spread like wings over tiny, close-set eyes. It wouldn't have shocked me if he'd stretched out his arms, given them a flap or two, and glided right out the window. Except for a starched white shirt, he wore solid black from the neck down—close-fitting suit, narrow tie, cloth gloves, and spit-shined shoes under wool spats. Bare-headed, I'd have taken him for a mortician, but the visored cap made him a chauffeur. And I don't get chauffeurs.

The birdshot eyes swept the office left to right, gave Monte a brief, puzzled frown, then left the dog to settle a somber gaze on me. When he opened his trap to speak, there was nothing bird-like about the voice. Low and smooth, with a trace of faded British.

"Nate Ross, I presume?"

I passed on making a Stanley and Livingstone joke, or a couple of other smart remarks that sprang to mind. No point wasting my razor wit on a guy who didn't look like he'd appreciate it or even recognize it.

"That's me," I said. Not humorous but efficient. At the sound of my voice, Monte opened a sleepy eye and gave me a curious look as if to say, "What's with this guy?"

"My name is Spencer, sir. I am here with a request on behalf of my employer."

"And who's your employer?"

"I am not at liberty to say just now. My employer wishes you to accompany me so that you may confer in person."

"Accompany you where?"

"Again, Mr. Ross, I regret that I cannot say."

I couldn't decide whether to be more amused by this oddball or annoyed at the mystery man act. Normally, I'd have been more suspicious, but the guy looked harmless, and Monte, who has an instinct for a wrong character, hadn't so much as raised his head off his paws.

"Well, Buster," I said, waving a hand over the papers spread across my desk, "you can see I'm pretty busy. So I'd need a little more to go on before I could offer to do anything for you or your boss."

He stuck a hand inside his coat, and habit, rather than any real concern, made me reach toward the .380 in the open drawer at my elbow. But instead of a gat, he came out with a bulky envelope which he stepped forward and laid on the desk in front of me.

I picked it up and looked inside. I drew out a banded stack of bills and riffled through them. Twenty-five nice, crisp, hundred-dollar notes.

"Your fee, sir, simply for coming along with me and hearing my employer's proposal."

"On the level?"

"I beg your pardon?"

"What I mean," I hefted the envelope, "is this is serious cash. I don't hire out to do any shady business. So if that's what you're after—"

"Certainly not, sir." He looked at his watch. "Now, if we may, I'm expected back, and I do have other duties to attend to."

I thought it over for a minute. Curiosity, not to mention the twenty-five hundred cash, crowded out any suspicion. I locked the envelope in my desk, stood up, and grabbed my hat.

"Okay, bub, I'll come along and hear what's what. All right if I bring my dog?"

He looked at Monte and cleared his throat. "Really, sir, I think—"

"Never mind." I picked up the phone and called Gus's Diner downstairs. My pal, Benjy, Gus's nephew, was on duty and more than happy to look in on Monte while I was away.

The chauffeur went out, and before following him I took my .380 from the desk and holstered it, just in case.

* * *

Parked in the gravel lot, taking up most of the space between my building's entrance and Gus's Diner, was a sleek and shiny limousine. A Packard Twelve. If this was someone's idea of a gag, it was an elaborate one. If it was a hit, I was going to die in style. My solemn visitor opened the rear door with a flourish and stood aside for me to enter.

"Why don't I just follow you in my car?" I asked.

"My employer insists, Mr. Ross." He gestured toward the open door, and having no good argument come to mind, I climbed in and settled back in the cream-soft leather seat.

He closed the door and got in behind the wheel. The big engine gave a soft growl as he started it, then smoothed out and became almost noiseless. As we pulled out onto the street, I spotted Benjy watching open-mouthed from the diner's window. I gave him a jaunty salute but couldn't tell if he saw me.

Chapter Two

The drive into the hills was so smooth and quiet, and the backseat so snug and warm, that I could have fallen asleep if it weren't for my mind puzzling over this screwy business and trying to guess what it was all about. A sliding window separated me from the driver's seat, and it was shut, so I had no conversation at all from my strange companion. I recognized where we were until we reached Franklin Canyon, where we veered off onto what looked like a private road snaking its way back and forth up the hillside. The farther we went, the cleaner—and more expensive—the air smelled.

We passed a sparse scattering of big houses that gave way to mansions, and before long came to what I assumed was the entrance to an estate, though there was no house yet in sight. The grounds were surrounded by a golden-brown brick wall eight feet high, with the entrance being a tall wrought iron gate set into an archway made of the same brick. As we approached, the gate automatically swung open, and we passed on through. It swung closed behind us, and we glided up a long, winding path flanked with eucalyptus trees. We topped a low rise, and I caught my first sight of the house, a stately, English country-style manor of the same blond brick with chimneys at its four corners. The house itself must have spread over at least half an acre.

My driver glided the big car up the gravel drive and stopped at a wide porte-cochere. He came around to my door and seemed disconcerted when I opened it and got out on my own. I looked the place over with what I figured was the expected awe and even threw in a low whistle for fun.

"So this is your employer's place?"

"It is, sir."

"And what happens now?"

Before he could respond, the huge front door opened, and a short, stout woman stepped out without a word. She wore a bib apron over a black frock, and her iron-gray hair was pulled tightly back into an uncomfortable looking bun. Black eyes glittered behind steel-rimmed nose glasses and above a straight slash of a mouth. She looked, if possible, even more humorless than the chauffeur.

"This is Mrs. Borne, the housekeeper," he said. "She will show you into the house." He stood straight, and I half expected him to click his heels as he touched his cap. "I will conduct you back to your place of business as you require, sir." He marched back around to the driver's door, slid in, and drove away. To where I couldn't see.

"This way, if you please," said Mrs. Borne. She had a more youthful and pleasant voice than the severe looks promised. I followed her down a long, surprisingly sparse hallway and into a large room made bright by wall sconces and floor-to-ceiling French windows lining one wall. They looked out over a stretch of smooth, green lawn that would have made a respectable airfield. A tall woman in khaki slacks and a black turtleneck sweater stood looking out the windows. Her back was to me, and all I could see was that she had a trim figure and long, wavy, white gold hair.

"Mr. Ross to see you, Miss Chase," the housekeeper said. She backed out and closed the door behind her. The woman at the window turned and stepped my way, extending a polite hand.

"Mr. Ross, how do you do?" She didn't bother introducing herself. She didn't have to.

Audrey Chase was Hollywood's latest oomph girl. Not that anyone in town—probably including herself—chalked her success up to an excess of talent. It mainly owed itself to other attributes, inborn qualities she couldn't take any credit for, but that she had in spades and knew how to use to their full advantage. Nature had gifted her with a face made for the camera. It was as pure and as innocent as an angel's in a Renaissance painting. Her smooth, perfect skin glowed on celluloid. Eyes the color of Delft china dazzled in black and white; in Technicolor, they were electric. The platinum waves that framed the flawless face were a shade no bottled concoction could produce, and the way she filled out her wardrobe both above and below the waistline was enough to tempt even the most hidebound, churchified male down a path of prurient thoughts. I have the same red blood in my veins as any of those guys, and fewer of their scruples, so I had to struggle to keep my own head out of the cumulus as I shook the slender hand and mumbled something that sounded vaguely like words. She waved me to a chair and sat in another across from me. The whisper of silk stockings when she crossed her legs did nothing to help keep my feet planted on terra firma.

She was clearly used to that sort of reaction. She regarded me with a gentle smile that almost hid her amusement and waited for me to collect my thoughts and recall how to use speech. Even in my fogged state, I thought I could detect sadness or concern behind the smile.

"I appreciate your coming, Mr. Ross. I'm so sorry for all the mystery. I'd have come to your office myself but… Well, I think you can understand."

"How can I help you, Miss Chase?" I managed to get out, sounding—in my head at least—like a twelve-year-old boy.

She leaned in and hit me full on with those blues, and I felt my mouth going dry again. I did my best to ignore it and focus, because now I could clearly see worry in her eyes.

"It's my sister. I'm afraid she's been taken."

"Taken?"

"Kidnapped."

"I see. Ransom demand?"

She nodded. "A note was left at the front gate. It said that if I paid two thousand dollars, Beth would be freed in two days."

"Two thousand dollars?" I didn't say it outright, but that seemed like chump change to ask for from a movie star. "Why the return in two days?"

"I have no idea. They didn't say."

"And when are the two days up?"

"Yesterday."

"So you've already paid, but she hasn't been returned?"

"Yes." She started to choke up. "And I'm so worried. There were threats made, and—"

I held up a hand. "Let's not think the worst just yet. There could be plenty of reasons for that." I handed her a handkerchief, and she dabbed at her eyes. "Why don't you just start at the beginning. First, tell me about your sister. Beth, you said? How old is she?"

"Elizabeth—Beth. She's just turned eighteen. Her—" She started crying again. "Her birthday was two days ago."

"And she lives here with you?"

She sniffled and nodded. "Well," she said, "on the grounds. I've cared for her since our parents died ten years ago. She's in her last year of high school."

"What did you mean 'she lives on the grounds'?"

"Just that she doesn't actually stay here in the main house. Not full-time, that is. There's a cottage at the back of the property. She moved her things out there back when things were…unpleasant… with my ex-husband." She reddened a little at the mention of her former husband. I didn't read the gossip columns, but her divorce from Griffin Glenn a couple of years earlier, and all the high drama that came with it, had landed on page one of every rag in town.

"Okay, I said." I didn't want to get off track. "Tell me in detail what's happened. How was Beth taken?"

"We don't know. Spencer went to pick her up from school on Friday—she attends Hollywood High—and she wasn't there. I called her best friend, but Beth wasn't with her either. She did say she'd seen Beth at lunchtime. She didn't come home that night, and the next morning Spencer found the note fixed to the front gate."

"What time was this?"

"A little after seven."

"Where's the note now?"

"It's over here." She led me to a desk along the far wall. The note was tucked into the corner of the blotter.

"Only you and Spencer have touched this?" She nodded. "Bare hands?"

She shook her head. "I don't think so. Spencer wears gloves as part of his uniform, and I was dressed to go out."

I bent and studied the note. It was a single sheet of cheap stationery, creased across the middle where it had been folded. The penciled message was written in neat block letters. It read:

Audrey Chase,

We have your sister. She is unharmed. Tonight at 8 bring an envelope with $2,000.00 in unmarked bills to Pool's Sandwiches at Sunset and Vine. Tape the envelope under the seat of the stool closest to the pay phone and leave it. If you do as we say, you will get your sister back on Monday. No funny business and no cops or press – or else.

I tore a page from my pocket notebook, folded it around the note, and stuck them both in my breast pocket.

As we moved back to our seats, I asked, "Where were you headed?"

"I beg your pardon?"

"Saturday morning. You were dressed to go out at seven. Where to?"

"Is that pertinent?"

"It may or may not be. If someone has taken your sister, odds are they've been watching her. And you."

I tapped the pocket with the note in it. "They obviously know where you live. There could be a clue in your movements, your routine. Probably not, but maybe."

She sighed. "All right. If you must know, I was going to visit the *Times* office. One of their reporters had contacted me about some horrid accusations." Before I could ask, she went on. "Nothing with any bearing on this matter, I can assure you. Simply the price of fame in Hollywood, I'm afraid."

I decided to let the question ride. For now. "So what happened after you got the note?"

"We followed their instructions to the letter."

"Meaning you didn't notify the police?"

"They explicitly warned against it. And I was so afraid that…" She started to tear up again. "Anyway, I thought that I should seek some professional advice first."

"And you haven't heard from them since? No notes, no phone calls?"

She shook her head. "And no sister." She sobbed and used a little more of my handkerchief on her eyes.

I leaned back and pretended I was mulling over the problem. And I was, but not in the way she would expect. A few things bothered me about this tale. The ransom was too low. The two-day delay made no sense. And now her line about "professional advice." My experience was that people in her circle of so-called society tended to rate private eyes in the same class as pimps and bootleggers.

I watched her for a few seconds while she composed herself. The worry seemed genuine, but she *was* an actress. Not the top talent in town, maybe, but still a pro. And the two oldest publicity gags in Tinseltown were the fake threat of death or bodily harm and the bogus kidnapping. Usually, the money demand in those grifts came to an agent or some studio stiff, so this would be a new wrinkle. But I'd long since stopped being surprised by anything that happened in Hollywood.

I decided to play it out for now. I'd been paid plenty just to come and hear the story. I may as well do a little poking and see where it led. She had put her brave face back on and was looking expectantly at me.

"You say Spencer found the note?"

"Yes. He was going out for gasoline before driving me downtown."

"Is Spencer his first or last name?"

Her face went blank. "I really have no idea." She shook her head. "He's always just been *Spencer*."

"How long has he worked for you?"

"I don't understand what that had to do—" The perfect eyebrows went up. "Oh, I see. About nine years in all. He was my husband's driver before..."

"I'm assuming he made the money drop for you?" She nodded. "Were you along for the ride?"

"I waited in the car. And went back with him at midnight to check. The money was gone."

"Okay. Well, I'll want to talk to him when we're done here."

"Of course. He'll need to drive you back in any case." She bit her lip. "But surely you don't think—"

"Not really. I just need to get the details from his side. I'll need to look over the cottage, too."

"But if Beth was taken from school..." The blue eyes narrowed and cooled a few degrees. "Now I understand. What if this is all some pathetic ploy for publicity?" She stared me down for a good five seconds, then looked away. "I suppose I can't blame you for thinking it, considering..." She looked at me again. "I am *not* my ex-husband."

I held my hand up in a peace gesture. "I'm not implying that. I just need to start with all the information I can, consider all possibilities." But now that that possibility was out in the open, I could ask. "How about Beth? Any Hollywood ambitions—following in your footsteps?"

She barked a laugh. "Hardly. Very much the opposite. There was a time when I tried to encourage her—she's a beautiful girl. But with Griffin, I think she saw the ugly side of our business."

"Speaking of Griffin, how do I reach him?"

"Oh, now he's a bastard, but he would never do something like this. He and Beth doted on one another. His parting shot to me was telling me that he's left her everything in his will." Her lips twisted in a bitter smile. "She'll have a disappointment coming there."

"How's that?"

She turned palms up. "From what I hear, he's virtually penniless. Drinking, gambling, and women are expensive hobbies, and for an actor whose last picture was nearly a decade ago... As they say, in Hollywood, it doesn't matter who you *were*, only who you *are*."

"Sounds to me like a dandy motive for a quick score." She started to make another protest, and I held up a hand again. "All possibilities. I need to size him up for myself. Don't worry—if he doesn't know what's doing, he won't hear it from me. And we can mark him off the list."

She still looked uncertain, but she nodded. "I can give you the last address I have for Griffin. I can't guarantee it's current. What else can I do for now?"

I told her the main thing was to ring me right away if the kidnappers contacted her. I gave her the office phone, my home number, and the number at the Buscadero, my pal Dusty Vanner's bar and my unofficial second office.

I got a few essentials from her besides Glenn's address. She gave me a photo of Beth, and she was right—the girl was a beauty. Dead ringer for her sister, maybe fifteen years ago. She gave me a phone number and an address for Delia Morgan, the friend of Beth's she'd talked to. She denied there was any boyfriend in the picture. Looking at the girl's photo, I doubted that, but I kept it to myself.

She asked about fees, and I told her we could hash that out later. I'd already gotten a pretty sweet amount just for hearing her out, and she wasn't the type I'd have to chase down to collect a bill. Plus, I still wanted a little more convincing before I obligated myself.

She called Mrs. Borne to show me the cottage, and we said our goodbyes.

* * *

As I followed the housekeeper down the cobbled path across the wide, sloping green, I thought over my talk with Audrey Chase. I hoped I hadn't sounded like a starry-eyed schoolboy. As for her story, I still wasn't convinced. Maybe it was my natural suspicion of anything Hollywood, but the whole thing felt screwy. Then again, I'd been well paid, with no doubt more to come. I could always bow out later if I found out I was being played for a sap. And if this thing was on the up and up, I'd want to do what I could to bring the girl home safe.

The little cottage sat in a shaded back corner of the property, facing, but barely in sight of, the main house. Stunted oaks hemmed it in on two sides, and behind it ran the brick wall that surrounded the estate. I noticed a heavy, iron-studded door, framed with vines, set in the wall and connecting it with the outside world.

With a disapproving look at me, Mrs. Borne opened the door. She stood like a sentry beside it as I went in. Maybe afraid I might swipe some of the knick-knacks. At least she didn't plan to bird-dog me while I searched the place.

The inside was done up in a different style from the big house. The furnishings were all blond wood and brightly patterned chintz – feminine, but not ritzy. A few books and magazines were scattered about—*Collier's*, *National Geographic*—and some slim volumes full of airy-fairy poetry and assorted hooptedoodle. Not a *Variety* or *Hollywood Reporter* in sight.

I didn't find anything of interest in the small living room or the tiny, evidently unused corner kitchen. The bedroom and bathroom proved a little more promising. The closet held fewer clothes than I'd have expected a girl of Beth Chase's means to own. Several empty hangers dangled among the dresses and blouses. There were a couple of gaps in the shoe rack, and I saw no luggage at all.

Buff carpeting, thick and soft as sheepskin, covered the floor. Underneath the bedside table, it displayed the imprint of a pair of male shoes. In the bathroom sink, I found whiskers around the drain plug. Either Audrey Chase had lied to me, or there had been hanky-panky going on she didn't know about. I was inclined to believe the latter.

I found Mrs. Borne still standing her post just outside. "Quite finished, sir?" she asked with forced politeness. "If you'll follow me back to the house, I'll fetch Spencer to drive you."

"Actually, can you ask Spencer to meet me here?"

She half opened her mouth in protest but thought better of it. "If you like, sir." She moved to lock the door.

"And if you'd leave me the key, I'll have him return it to you."

She handed it over with a show of reluctance. "Will you require anything else?"

"I just have a question. Who has keys to that door in the outer wall?" I hitched a thumb toward the back of the cottage.

She pursed her lips. "Myself, Mr. Sims, the gardener, Spencer. And Miss Chase, of course."

"What about Beth?"

"Miss Elizabeth? Not to my knowledge, no."

I thanked her, and with one more distasteful look, she turned and walked toward the house. Spencer showed up not ten minutes later, skimming the big Packard along a driving path just inside the wall. I waited for him at the cottage door. If he was curious why I'd had him come out here, his face didn't show it.

"Shall I drive you back now, sir?" he asked when he'd walked up the little path.

"First, I'd like to ask you something. Come on inside."

He followed me in, and I led him to the bedroom and showed him the shoe prints under the table.

"Who is he?"

He gave me a blank look. "I beg your pardon, sir?"

"You can skip the British duty and honor bit, pal." I'd never known a chauffeur who didn't know all the family secrets. "You drive this girl to school and back every day—other places too, I'm guessing. I've been hired to find her, and whether she's been kidnapped or has run away or is just hiding out, I need to talk to anybody who might know something. Part of your duty is to her, too, right?"

The stone face cracked a little. "She didn't wish her sister to know."

"Why not?"

"She feared Miss Chase's disapproval. Apparently, the young man is the son of a housekeeper."

I tried to stifle a laugh. "That would be a disqualifier?"

"Miss Chase has a certain image to maintain. She's quite careful in that regard."

Hollywood. It never changes.

"Who is this lowly housekeeper's kid?"

He hesitated. "I trust I may count on your discretion, sir?"

"As far as it goes. I don't promise I'll keep the information from Miss Chase, but you've got my word I won't tell her how I learned it."

"Very well. His name is James. He and Miss Elizabeth are classmates."

"Last name?"

"I'm afraid I don't know."

"Okay, come on, you can tell me the rest on the way back to my office."

We climbed into the big bus, and as Spencer eased us away, I opened the sliding window. "Does young Jimmy by any chance have a key to the cottage?" I pointed "Or to that door in the wall?"

"I really couldn't say, sir. I suppose… I suppose it's not unlikely that Miss Elizabeth has furnished him one, for the door gate at least."

"How long have the lovebirds been carrying on?"

"Some months now."

"And the sister had no idea?"

"Miss Elizabeth has been quite discreet. They've met when Miss Chase supposed her to be going to music lessons or attending school functions."

He looked sadly at me in the rear-view mirror. "But I assure you, I had no idea that he was actually coming onto the grounds." His voice went morose. "Had I known, I might have…"

"Young love finds a way, Spencer."

I thought a change of subject was in order. "Why don't you tell me about this note you found?"

We spent most of the drive going over the details. He'd been on his way out to gas the Packard and had found the note folded and wedged between the bars of the front gate. He assumed at first it was some sort of message from a crew who'd been trimming trees along the private road. He did have his gloves on. It was early morning, but the paper was dry, so it hadn't been there long.

He immediately took the note to Audrey Chase. After a phone call or two—he didn't know who she'd called—she told him to keep the whole business under his hat. They hadn't discussed it any further until this morning, when she sent him to fetch me.

The basics out of the way, Spencer grew quiet again. A little too quiet, I thought. I waited a few minutes, then asked him, "Are you going to spill it, or what?"

He angled his chin slightly my way. "Sir?"

"Can it, Jeeves. You keep sneaking peeks at me in the mirror. I'm not pretty enough to warrant all that attention, so if there is something you're itching to say, say it. All that ogling is giving me the willies."

"Really, sir." The *really* stretched out longer than the car.

"Yes, *reaaally*." I tried to match him vowel for vowel. "No need to overwork the accent, it's just us two here." His ears reddened, and in the rear view, I saw his shaggy brows nuzzle each other. His jaw made a couple of false starts before he spoke.

"It's only…only that… It's not my place, I know. But if I may, I would suggest you look carefully at Mr. Glenn."

"As a possible kidnapper, you mean?"

He nodded. "His divorce from Miss Chase was most acrimonious. He left quite embittered, and I believe there were veiled threats."

"What sort of threats?"

"Vague promises to 'get even,' I believe, was the phrase used."

"Okay, that's worth knowing. Now, tell me—since you know these people, and I don't—any chance this whole thing is just a publicity grab?"

The bird-like eyes hardened, his voice went steely. "Certainly not. Miss Chase is at the top of her profession. She has no reason to resort to such tawdry tactics. In any case, she's an honorable woman."

"All right, it's just a question—there's no need to go choosing dueling pistols over it. Like I told her, I have to consider every angle. Besides, I was thinking more about publicity for the ex-husband. If I recall, he's pulled this kind of stunt in the past."

"I should not consider that entirely out of his character."

"Well, it sounds to me like I need to have a word with Mr. Glenn, then. First, I need to find out where he hangs his hat. Your boss seems to think the address she has is no good."

Just then, he pulled into the lot below my office. We stopped, and he sprang out and fairly sprinted around the car, but I beat him to the door again. He made a pained face as I got out.

"It's okay, pal. I'm not the Duke of Buckingham."

"As you will." He took a notebook and pen from his pocket, scribbled something, and handed me the torn-out sheet. "Mr. Glenn's current address, sir."

I glanced at the paper and pocketed it. He caught my appraising glance.

"I've taken the liberty of loosely monitoring Mr. Glenn. For the ladies' sale."

I shook my head. "You're quite the dark horse, aren't you, Spencer?"

His eyes betrayed a slight twinkle. "Merely a loyal employee, sir."

"Sure, whatever you say. Well, thanks for the information. And the ride."

He inclined his head. "Will there be anything else, sir?"

"I guess not." As he turned to go, I said, "There is one more thing. Is Spencer your first or last name?"

He almost smiled. "It is indeed, Mr. Ross." With that, he slid behind the wheel, cranked up the big twelve, and drifted away.

Chapter Three

The address Spencer had given me for Griffin Glenn told me a lot. Before I'd even seen the place, I could judge how far the actor's fortunes had fallen. The house was on the fringes of Bunker Hill, a neighborhood that had once been home to some of the city's richest and had boasted some of its grandest, most opulent Victorian manors. But over the decades, the wealthy folks had died off or moved on, the houses had become frail, dilapidated ghosts of what they'd once been, and the district had mostly become home to down-and-outers. A perfect place for a has-been movie star to end up.

On the drive there, I went over what I knew about Griffin Glenn. I didn't much keep up with movieland news, but Glenn had often been front-page fodder, and seldom in a good way. He'd been a pretty boy actor back in the silent days—a sort of Yankee Valentino. He was blessed with a smooth baritone and perfect diction, so he'd been one of the fortunate few to switch over to talkies without his star losing any of its shine. He'd weathered the usual whispers and minor scandals, but they hadn't tarnished him much. If anything, they added luster. Things were fairly peachy for him until age crept in. The hair thinned, the face started showing lines that pancake couldn't quite hide anymore, and almost overnight he went from romantic lead to playing eccentric professors and doting fathers.

He'd gotten a brief boost in popularity with his very public courtship and marriage to a young and glamorous up-and-comer. But when Audrey Chase's star started to outshine his own, things turned ugly. Soon, the only press he got was for his latest gin-soaked brawl, pinch in a gambling raid, or lecherous pursuit of minor starlets—at least one of them *minor* in both senses of the word. The public spectacle of his divorce from Audrey Chase hadn't worked in his favor. The kicker came when he tried to drum up a little public sympathy by claiming he had gotten letters and phone calls threatening to throw acid in his once handsome mug if he didn't come across with a hefty payment. The cops wasted a week on it before they determined it was all bunk. The guy hadn't even had sense enough to dump the typewriter he'd written the phony notes on. He'd used up the last of his markers to stay out of jail, and since then, he was pure poison in Hollywood. Nobody was going to hire him to dump wastebaskets on a set.

Audrey Chase had said she didn't believe Glenn could be involved in this caper, but she also hadn't mentioned he'd made any threats. One of the first lessons I learned as a young copper was that everybody holds back, everybody lies, even people who are supposed to be on your side. She had warned me, however, that Glenn was not likely to be very helpful or cooperative.

I'd had a picture in my head of what the guy's house would be like and was surprised to find it less shabby than expected. It was nothing compared to the digs he'd shared with his former wife, but for a guy who was by all accounts on the skids, it wasn't so bad.

For starters, most of these old houses had been split up into apartments. But at Glenn's address, I saw only one mailbox and no numbers tacked up by any of the doors. He was evidently the lone occupant. The paint was faded, the woodwork dry and cracked, and the grass was sepia-tinted and slightly overgrown, but overall the house looked clean and in decent repair.

I stepped up into the shade of the railed front porch and was about to put knuckles to the wide oak door when I spotted a brass doorbell to one side. I gave that a try instead. I heard a muffled chime from inside but got no answer. I tried again after a while, and a third time half a minute later. Nothing. I stepped off the porch and checked the flap-top mailbox nailed to one of the newel posts. There were three or four pieces of mail in it—probably a day or two's worth at most. None of it interested me.

I decided to take a good look around the outside while I debated whether to tickle the lock and go through the place. I'd noticed a carriage house toward the back that looked like it had been converted to a garage—as good a place as any to start. I walked along a narrow driveway paved with broken and uneven brick, and when I reached the back of the house, I heard a distinct buzzing noise. It didn't take long to pinpoint it. A wooden stairway ran along the house's rear wall from a door on the upper floor. At the bottom of the stairs, lying half in, half out of a dried-up flower bed, was a body.

I didn't need to check for signs of life. The greenish pallor and the unnatural angle of the head were enough. The flies hadn't done much damage yet to the bloated face, so I still recognized it from the photos I had seen. Griffin Glenn, all right.

He was fully dressed, and his clothing was disarranged and smudged a bit. One arm was tucked under him, and one stretched out above his head. Two of the fingers on that hand were broken or dislocated, and he had a large, discolored goose egg on one side of his forehead. I didn't see any other obvious injuries. It looked as though he'd taken a tumble down the stairs and broken his neck. I judged he'd been dead not much more than a day.

Six inches from the outstretched hand, a whiskey bottle lay in the dead grass. An ounce or so was left in it. Besides the expected smell, the body stank of the stuff. Careful not to disturb the body, I probed in his pockets until I found a ring of keys. I was guessing I'd find the door at the top of the stairs unlocked, but I didn't want to destroy any footprints—or leave any.

I went to a side door that led into the kitchen and tried the keys until I found one that fit. I spent an hour or so going through the house top to bottom. I didn't find any kidnapped girls or any sign that anyone but Glenn had occupied the place. I found plenty of empty bottles, and walls hung with lithographed posters of Glenn's films and framed photos from his salad days. I only came across a couple of items of any interest. One was a typewriter sitting on a card table in the living room. I wondered if it was the same one he'd banged out his fake threat notes on. I didn't find any stationery that matched Audrey Chase's note.

The other item was a bank book I found in the top dresser drawer in his bedroom. Monthly deposits of five hundred dollars were recorded in it, going back more than a year. Glenn clearly had some regular—or *irregular*—source of income, though I didn't find anything to give me a clue as to what that might be.

Much as I hated to, I was going to have to call the police. Glenn had a phone, but I didn't want to put them wise that I'd been in the house, so I drove to a corner drugstore a couple of blocks away and dropped a nickel in their payphone. I drove back to the house and waited in my car. I sat and smoked for fifteen minutes until a city car drove up and a pair of patrol coppers got out.

I led them around to the body, and they asked the usual questions about why I was there and got the usual unsatisfactory answers. They were both slicksleeves and fairly young pups, so I didn't have to endure the hostility my name normally triggered in the local gendarmerie. I knew I wasn't likely to be as fortunate when the detectives showed up.

I was almost relieved when the big black sedan rolled up, and Carl Queenan stepped out of the passenger seat. I didn't recognize the driver . Queenan was a captain of Homicide and one of the few old timers who didn't hold my past sins against me. That hadn't always been the case. But we'd had enough dealings over time that he was usually pretty reasonable. It still didn't stop him from making the occasional threat on my freedom or my life, but I wasn't expecting either from him in this case.

"Top of the mornin', Ross." He looked at his watch. "Or afternoon, I guess. What kind of hijinks are we up to today?"

Right away, my spirits sank a little. Queenan was normally gruff and grumpy when we bumped into each other. Whenever he gave me a friendly greeting, it put me on my guard.

"Hello, Cap. Isn't your desk chair going to get cold without your fanny to warm it?"

"Aw, you know me. When I hear Nate Ross is calling one in, I can't resist coming out for a look-see. What have you got that's going to ruin my nice, quiet day?"

The two uniforms looked a little sour that he had addressed the question to me and not to them. The older of the two spoke up.

"Dead guy in the backyard, Cap. Looks to me accidental-like, but I guess you'll be the judge."

"Lead on, boys, lead on." Queenan dropped his cigar stub in the gutter and lit a fresh one from his pocket.

As we all walked to the backyard, Queenan turned to the other detective, a lanky, sad-faced guy about my age. "Where's my manners? Clyde, this is Nate Ross, private eye. You wanna watch yourself—he's slicker than Sam Spade and shoots quicker and straighter than Race Williams. Ross, this here is Clyde Decker."

"How do you do?" Decker said. He didn't offer to shake hands, but I thought nothing of that. Cops weren't big on the social niceties. If my name meant anything to him, he didn't show it.

We hovered over the body while they both studied the layout. Decker squatted down for a closer look, winced a little at the smell. He looked up at me. "Found him just like this? You didn't move him at all?"

"Haven't touched him," I half-lied.

Queenan gave a little grunt that could have meant anything or nothing. I knew what it meant.

Decker went through the dead man's pockets, pulled out a wallet, and looked inside. He took another gander at the face. "I'll be damned. I thought he looked a little familiar." He handed the wallet to Queenan.

Queenan read the license and gave a short laugh. "Well, what do you know? Mr. Acid-in-the Puss himself. Guess his career's dead for good now."

Decker pulled out Glenn's keys from the pocket I'd returned them to. He looked up the stairway, then back at me. "That door up there locked?"

I shrugged. "Couldn't tell you. I didn't think I should go up the stairs." He stared at me for a moment, then nodded. He stood up.

"Guess we'd better have a look inside, Cap."

"You get started," Queenan said. "I don't want to drop cigar ash in the house. I'll be along."

Decker looked at Queenan, me, and Queenan again. He nodded once more and turned without a word, motioning to the two patrol coppers to follow. They all disappeared around the corner.

Queenan stared at the body and puffed his cigar for a long while. I waited.

I knew what was coming.

"What do you make of it, Ross?" he said at last.

"What do *you* make of it, Cap?"

"All right, I'll play. Looks to me like some party or other tried to get cute here." He pointed at the whiskey bottle with the toe of a shoe. "We're supposed to buy that he held on to that while he tumbled down the stairs. Hell, it ain't even cracked." He leaned over and sniffed. "And I don't care how much the guy guzzled, he wouldn't stink that much of booze unless someone soaked him with it." He looked at me. "You see it any different?"

I shook my head.

"Pretty clear he *did* fall down the stairs, though. What do you think—pushed or tossed?"

"Hard to say," I told him.

He gazed up the stairway. "Don't see any damage to that door or the railing. For now, my money's on *pushed*."

I just nodded. He was taking his time getting to the point.

"So what did you find?" *There* it was. Before I could answer, he said, "Don't even try giving me those innocent Nate Ross eyes. Don't spoil my good mood. But before you tell me what you found when you tossed the house, start by telling me how you come to be here in the first place."

"I was hired to find a girl—probably a runaway. You know I can't tell you who, or who hired me. Not without the client's okay." I looked down at Glenn. "There was a chance he might know something about it, so I came to see him. This is what I found."

He shook his head. "You know, the favors I do you, you could do me one every now and then."

"I've done plenty of favors for you, Cap, when I could."

He gave me the dog eye and backhanded the air. "Blah. So *you* say." He sighed. "All right, I'll let that go for now." He pointed his cigar at me like a gun. "But you talk to your client, 'cause I need to know what's what here," I told him I would. "Now, back to the other point. You find anything inside that might throw a little light on this?"

I told him about the bank book. I couldn't see any reason to hold that back.

"Okay, gimme." He held out a beefy hand.

"Give me some credit, Cap. I didn't take it." The door at the top of the stairs opened just then, and Decker leaned out to give the landing and stairs the once-over. "Besides, if this guy is any good, he's found it already."

"Of course he's good. He's one of mine." He looked at me again, this time with mock sympathy but a twinkle in his eye. "Tough luck for you, I hear. That Palomar caper."

Good mood or not, he could never pass up a chance to give me the razoo. I grinned back at him and tried to pretend that subject wasn't like a toothache to me. "Yeah, well, easy come, easy go."

"I guess." He took one last pull on his cigar and ground it out in the dirt. "I see the print boys are here. I better go see how they're coming. You can toddle off if you need to. We'll get you down on paper later." He started around toward the front of the house. At the corner, he glanced back at me, and I heard him chuckle.

* * *

When I got back to the office, it was nearly dark. Too late in the day to visit Audrey Chase, but I thought she should get the news in person. I was confident the news hounds weren't going to get the word of Glenn's death in time to get it into the morning edition, so I took Monte out for a break, then to Gus's for a bite of dinner, and we went on home.

Chapter Four

Next morning, I skipped breakfast and arranged to go out and see Audrey Chase. Traffic was light as I drove to the estate. Monte had thrown such a pitiful mope when I started to leave him home that I took him along.

"Best behavior, pal," I told him as Spencer opened the gate for us. "These people aren't used to scroungy mutts like us visiting them." I gave Spencer a quick salute as I rolled past him and up the long drive.

Mrs. Borne was waiting for us at the door. She was looking a little less disdainful of me this morning. She took immediate note of the big, furry head poking out the window, and I figured she'd be freshly disgusted.

"He'll be fine in the car," I assured her. "He's not much of a barker."

But the old lady surprised me with a slight smile. "You may bring him along if you'd like. Miss Chase has rather a fondness for dogs."

Just to be safe, I clipped on Monte's leash. Normally, he balks at that, but he seemed so fascinated by our surroundings, for once he didn't fuss.

* * *

"What a beautiful dog!" Audrey Chase said when we'd been shown into the spacious living room.

"This is Monte," I told her. "I hope it's okay."

"Of course. Is he trained for detective work?"

"I've been told more than once he's the brains of the outfit."

She laughed and offered me a seat on a long velvet sofa. Monte lay down at my feet, and she took a chair next to him. "Is it all right if I pet him?"

I said it was, and she gave his ears a ruffle. He immediately rolled onto his back for a belly rub. So she had that effect on animals, too.

She regarded him curiously. "What breed is he?"

"I'm not quite sure. Part German Shepherd, part buffalo, I suspect." She laughed again, and the big brute's tongue lolled as she stroked his belly fur. He was clearly in love.

After a moment, she looked up. "But I'm guessing you didn't come here just to introduce me to your dog."

As gently as I could, I told her about Griffin Glenn. I wasn't expecting any hysterics, and I didn't get any. No hysterics and no tears. She took the news quietly, with widened eyes and a hand to her mouth. I studied those big blue eyes and thought what I saw in them was relief.

"Thank you for bringing me the news," she said after a long pause. "It would have been a shock to read it in the newspaper."

"You're welcome," I said. "But there's a little more to it. I didn't tell the police exactly why I was there, but I may not be able to stall them for long."

"Police? I don't understand. If it was an accident..."

"That's just it. It looks as though it wasn't."

"You don't mean...murdered?"

"I'm afraid so."

That did it. She let out a violent breath, her eyes rolled back, and she started to pitch out of her chair. Monte gave a startled bark and scrambled out of the way as I lunged off the sofa and caught her. I lifted her off the chair and laid her on the sofa.

A door opened, and Mrs. Borne bustled in. "Is everything all right?"

"Miss Chase has fainted. Do you have any brandy?"

"Of course." The housekeeper disappeared and came back with a half-filled snifter. Her face was drawn. "What happened, Mr. Ross?"

I took the glass from her hand. "A little bad news," I said. Her face went a shade whiter, and the black eyes flashed horror. "Not Beth. Mr. Glenn's been killed." I hoped she wasn't going to keel over, too. One wingding at a time.

To my relief, she stayed upright. "How awful," she murmured. She reached out a hand and touched Audrey's arm as I lifted her head and held the glass to her lips. "Shall I call for a doctor?"

"Let's give it a minute," I said, tipping a little brandy into Audrey's half-opened mouth. "I think she'll be okay."

Audrey took an involuntary sip, coughed a little. Her eyes fluttered open and took a second to focus. She looked at me and Mrs. Borne in turn, then at the brandy snifter. She wrapped her fingers around mine on the glass and took a deep swallow of the stuff. After a moment, she sat up, smoothed her hair, and gave us both an embarrassed smile.

"I'm so sorry. Foolish of me." She noted Mrs. Borne's worried face and patted her hand. "I'm fine, Ada, really."

"Can I get you anything more, Miss Chase?"

Audrey swung her feet to the floor and sat upright. "No, thank you. I think all I need is some fresh air." She stood slowly, then turned to me. "Would you walk with me?"

"Sure."

Mrs. Borne took reluctant leave, and Audrey led me out through the French windows. We went to the right and into a large, well-tended rose garden. With Monte alongside, we strolled down a flagstone path underneath a long arbor canopied with bougainvillea.

After a long silence, she stopped and faced me. "Can I rely absolutely on your discretion, Mr. Ross? That you'll keep things I tell you in the strictest confidence?"

"It's Nate," I said. "And I won't mislead you—talking to me isn't exactly like talking to a priest or lawyer. There's no legal blanket for either of us. All I can give you is my word."

She studied my face for a long time. "Beth is my daughter," she said, almost in a whisper. She gave me a moment to soak that in, then we started walking again. "I was fifteen. Fifteen going on twenty, or so I thought. There was a boy at school—tall, handsome, two years older. I'll spare you the details—you can guess the rest. We lived in a small town in Michigan. My father was a doctor and a city councilman, and appearances mattered, you know? So, when they found out, it was decided that we would all take an extended trip abroad, after word was spread in our town that my mother was pregnant. And so for several years, I lived with a 'sister' until my parents were killed in a car crash and I found myself in the odd position of becoming a surrogate mother to my own child."

"Does Beth know?"

A bitter smile crossed her face. "Not from me. I hadn't decided whether I would ever tell her. But Griffin knew, and telling her was just one more way for him to strike out at me. You can imagine it's made things between Beth and me a little strained. It's the real reason she decided to live in the cottage."

"Is that why you're telling me this now?"

"Partly. But also because you should probably know that Griffin was blackmailing me. He was desperate for money, and he had something he knew I'd pay to keep quiet." She laughed a mirthless laugh. "We must keep up the image, and God knows, with Griffin I'd already had enough public humiliation. Anyway, it's bound to come out now. Griffin would have left signs."

"Five hundred dollars a month?" She stopped walking and shot me a startled look. "Entries in his bank book."

She nodded understanding and laid her hand on my arm. "But mostly, Nate, I'm telling you because I need you to fully understand how desperate I am to have Beth back and safe." Her eyes welled up, and her voice clogged. "She's all I have."

With that, the dam broke, and she fell to weeping and gasping for breath. Her shoulders heaved like the surf at high tide. Without warning, she grabbed handfuls of my coat, pulled in tight, and buried her face in my shirt front. I wrapped my arms around her shoulders and held her until the shakes subsided and her breathing settled down. If I'd had any doubts that her concern was on the level, they disappeared.

She took a half step back, wiped her eyes with both hands, and turned a faltering smile on me. "Forgive me. I know you didn't sign on to be my nursemaid."

"It's all right." I was about to offer her a handkerchief when she pulled one from the pocket of her slacks. As she blotted her eyes, I recognized it as the one I'd offered her on our first meeting.

We walked slowly back toward the house, talking over the situation with Beth. She had had no more notes, no phone calls, nothing to give her a clue whether Beth was alive or dead. I tried to reassure her that the abductors had probably just gotten greedy and decided they could tap her for more than a lousy two grand. In which case, they'd definitely be in touch soon. That seemed to ease her mind a little.

After the story she'd told me, I wasn't about to clue her in about Beth's boyfriend and shenanigans at the cottage. But I did decide my next move would be to look up this *James* and see what light, if any, he could shed on things. Because I still had the nagging suspicion this caper wasn't exactly what it appeared to be.

Back at the house, Audrey apologized again, thanked me for my understanding, and so on, and promised to call me the second any news broke. Instead of calling Mrs. Borne, she walked Monte and me to the front door. She squatted down and tousled the big mutt's fur.

"Goodbye, Monte. Come back and visit again, any time."

She stood, and as I was halfway out the door, she stepped forward and put a hand on my shoulder. When I turned, she mouthed a silent, small 'Thank you' then leaned in and gave me a quick kiss before closing the door. I tried not to let it affect me but couldn't help noticing a kind of lightness in my step as we walked to the car.

Chapter Five

I gave the plate a suspicious once-over as Dusty slid it in front of me. Since I'd missed breakfast and since I wanted to keep my mind on business and off things I shouldn't be thinking about, I'd stopped at the Buscadero to have lunch and to talk the case over with my pal.

The bar was quiet at midday. The horde of Hollywood cowpokes normally hanging about the place spent most of their daylight hours on film sets, toiling as wranglers, stuntmen, dog-kicking heavies, and other bit part players. Today, even Dusty's business partner, Pooter, was off on a movie job. So today the place was quiet as the public library. Just Dusty, Monte, and me.

I rotated the plate a half turn and stared at it. "What the hell is this?"

I'd asked him for the house specialty—a hamburger topped with cheese and chopped chilis. Next to the Gotham Deli's pastrami it was, for my money, the tastiest lunch in town. What Dusty gave me looked like a burger with its top bun off, smothered under a thick blanket of chili, cheese, diced onions, and a mound of chopped chili peppers.

"New item on the menu," Dusty said. "Chili size."

"*Size?* What's that mean?"

"It's what Ptomaine Tommy's calls it".

Ptomaine Tommy's has been a local institution since I was a kid. Name aside, I recalled the food being pretty good, though I hadn't eaten there since I was a teenager.

"But why chili *size?*"

"Tommy's got two chili ladles: a small one for toppin' burgers and a big one for bowls. Somehow he come up with the notion of servin' his hamburger open-faced and usin' the big ladle—the *chili-size* one—to cover it with chili."

"So you and Pooter just pinched his idea?"

He gave one end of his ridiculous handlebar mustache a tug. "Borrowed and improved. The peppers was Pooter's idea. And of course, we don't use no *gringo* chili."

I didn't have to ask what that crack meant. Pooter and Dusty, both native Texans, had strong opinions on what constituted 'real' chili. As far as they were concerned, anything with beans in it wasn't worth eating.

I wasn't about to admit to Dusty that the dish looked and smelled pretty good. "Okay," I said, "But how am I supposed to eat it?"

He held up a finger. "My apologies." He reached under the counter, then slapped a napkin-wrapped knife and fork next to my plate. "Your weapons, sir."

He looked at Monte, who was perched on the next stool, paws on the bar, eyeballing my meal. "How about you, *amigo*?"

I swallowed the first bite. Even better than it smelled. "Set him up with the same, only no chili or onions and definitely no peppers."

"Pooter's toned the chili down for the burgers—the peppers got heat enough."

"Maybe, but I don't need the office fumigated."

"Okey dokey, one burger with cheese, sans fixin's, comin' right up."

He disappeared through the swinging doors, and I heard kitchen noises and off-key humming while I ate and washed the food down with beer. He came back a few minutes later carrying an open-faced burger topped with grated cheese on a plate.

Monte hopped down and met him halfway across the floor. He pounced on the plate and gobbled his burger down in the time it took me to carve off another chunk of mine. Then he rolled over and went to sleep.

Dusty took the dog's vacated seat. "Sorry to hear that Palomar case didn't work out for you," he said.

With my mouth full, I just gave him a noncommittal shrug. It was a sore subject, and he knew it. He watched me closely as I chewed and swallowed. When he saw I wasn't going to take the bait, he switched topics.

"So what brings you around today? You never come in just for food or drink. Or conversation, for that matter. What's on your mind?"

I gave him a quick rundown of the case so far. Dusty was a former lawman and had assisted me on more than one occasion, so I didn't have to worry about him keeping my business under his ten-gallon hat.

He listened without comment and when I finished asked in his usual laconic way, "Believe her?"

"As far as it goes. The worry's no act, I'm sure of that. That doesn't mean it's not still some Hollywood bullshit. It could be that someone else cooked up a stunt without her knowing. Her agent, the studio—who knows? Hell, her ex-husband pulled a similar gag not all that long ago."

"The dead fella?" I nodded. "But you're takin' it on anyhow?"

"Yeah, well, there's always the chance it's on the level." I took a sip of my beer, "Plus, the money's more than I'd make in half a year. And as it is…" I stopped myself. I wasn't going to give him the chance to needle me about the Palomar again.

He flashed a quick, knowing grin under his mustache. "What's that you're always sayin' about money?"

"This isn't all about the money." It sounded more snappish than I intended. He threw his hands up in surrender, and we sat in silence while I finished my food. "What's your gut read on it?" he asked at last.

"I'm not sure that baby sister hasn't just taken it on the run. There's a boyfriend in the mix, and they've been playing hide-the-pickle right under the sister's nose." I was careful to say *sister*. I was keeping that part of the story to myself—I wasn't going to give away Audrey's secret.

"Anyway," I said, dabbing at my mouth with a napkin, "I'll probably need some help on it. Especially if, or when, she gets another demand."

He grimaced. "Pooter's expectin' to be gone several days, so I'm pretty much tied down here till he's back. What about that little red-headed fella—Danny, was it?"

"Danny's all right for tail jobs and basic leg work. Headwork, he's not so reliable. You think Walt would be interested?"

"Sorry. He's in Arizona windin' up a couple of cases while he's waitin' to take the bar out here."

As though L.A. needed more lawyers. "Is he going to stick with probate?"

"He's thinkin' criminal work might suit him better."

"Well, he ought to find no shortage of clients." I finished my beer, stood up, and pushed the plate away. I stifled a belch. "Okay, you've made me a believer. But you've got to come up with a catchier name than *chili size.* I mean, this *is* Hollywood."

"I was thinking maybe *Busky Burger.*"

"Now you're talking." Monte was still motionless in his spot on the floor, softly snoring. "Since you're leaving me on my own, mind if I leave the mutt here for a while? I've got some nosing around to do."

"Fine with me. He's good company." He stood up. "Before you go, though..." He leaned over and opened the cash register, took out some change, "You've been complainin' we don't play nothin' but cowboy tunes. So I loaded some new records in the box." He went over to the big Symphanola jukebox, dropped in a nickel, and punched a button. "Here's one you might fancy."

I listened as the machine buzzed and whirred, then gave out with a few opening notes I recognized. Count Basie's *Blues in the Dark.*

I gave him my best go-to-hell look. "Why do I even talk to you?"

He laughed and gave my shoulder a punch. "Sorry, Nate. Just couldn't resist." As I walked to the door, he said, "Say, give me a call if you get in a fix. I'll see what I can do."

Chapter Six

Hollywood High was over on Highland. Spencer hadn't been able to tell me where the boyfriend lived, but with school in session, I'd decided to try my luck there. If, as I suspected, he wasn't in class I'd at least get an address.

Just my luck—the passing bell rang as I walked in, and I had to wade through a tidal wave of chattering girls and blustering boys, the boys throwing catcalls and wolf whistles at the girls while playing grab-ass with each other. I couldn't remember being such an idiot at their age. Wishful thinking, no doubt.

I'd brought along an item I seldom used. How my old man came to have it, I never knew and probably didn't want to. It was a "juice badge"—a sort of honorary badge the L.A.P.D. had doled out to certain influential parties a couple of police chiefs ago. If it wasn't examined too closely, it gave the impression the bearer was a detective with the L.A.P.D. As a rule, I tried not to break too many laws before dinnertime, but it was the surest way I could think of to get what I needed without tipping my mitt.

I flashed the buzzer at a plump secretary parked at a scarred, overflowing desk behind a low, gated partition like the ones in courtrooms. She was on the phone and started to raise a wait-a-minute finger, but when she saw the tin, she made a hasty excuse and hung up. It hadn't sounded like a business call, anyway.

She straightened a little, put on her professional face, and peered up at me through harlequin glasses.

"Good afternoon, officer. How may I help you?"

"I need to speak with Mr. Duffy." I'd clocked the principal's photo and brass nameplate on the wall in the corridor. Plus, the frosted glass in the door over her shoulder was lettered "Milton Duffy – Principal" in flaking gold letters. I'm all kinds of wily.

She smiled politely. "May I tell him what this is in reference to?"

"Just tell him it's official business."

She didn't like that. The smile dissolved, but she punched a button on her phone, and I heard a faint buzz behind the door. She relayed my message, and I could hear a muffled, tinny reply. She hung up and looked back up at me with a stiff smile. "Go right in."

I nodded thanks. I had to wrestle the gate a little before the latch clicked open. It seemed to amuse her.

* * *

Principal Duffy stood up behind his desk as I walked in. His photo outside made him look imposing, but he was only slightly taller standing than sitting. Still, he was a stern-looking bird, so I was a little surprised by his jovial greeting.

"Good afternoon, sir! Here to sell me tickets to the Policeman's Ball?" He made a feint for his wallet and laughed. I almost came back with the old joke from my sheriff's department days that L.A. coppers don't have balls, but considered that a school principal might not be the most appreciative audience.

"Not today, I'm afraid," was all I said.

He dropped the fake heartiness and looked concerned. "Serious business, then?"

"Well, nothing that threatens life or limb. I'm looking for a witness."

He offered me a chair, and I sat with my hat on my knee. He took his own seat again. "A witness to what?"

"A crime I'm investigating. I can't really say more than that—you understand."

"Of course, of course." The cagey line generally worked. People like to be

37

part of a secret, even if they aren't really in on it. "Can you tell me—is it a staff member or student?"

"A student. My problem is that I only know his first name—James, or maybe Jimmy." I gave him Spencer's sketchy description of the kid. It probably fit half a dozen boys he knew, so I hit him with the kicker. "If it helps, another witness told me the boy's friends with a girl named…" I pretended to consult my notebook, "Elizabeth Chase."

I could see the light switch flick on in his head. The worried face returned. "I hope Miss Chase isn't involved in anything…untoward."

I shook my head and smiled. "Not at all. Nice girl, is she?"

"She is that," he said with some relief. "She's also the younger sister of Audrey Chase."

"Ah," I said, throwing in a wink. "I get it. No need to worry on that score. It's the boy I'm looking for. I take it you know who I mean?"

He nodded. "I believe James Singer would be your man. Fine young fellow. Throws a heck of a fastball. He and Beth have been chummy for some time now."

I tried not to smile at *chummy*, but he caught my look. "I can guess what you're thinking." He grinned. "There are no secrets on a high school campus."

I didn't tell him how far *that* guess missed the mark. Instead, I gave him another wink, and he reached for his desk phone.

"Mrs. Hooper, would you have James Singer sent in?" He listened a moment, frowned, "I see. Could you send for Elizabeth Chase then?" More listening and frowning. A couple of "Mm hmms," and he hung up.

"I'm very sorry, Officer…"

"DeMasse. Paul DeMasse." It was my usual moniker when I needed one. My private joke—an anagram of *Samuel Spade*.

"Officer DeMasse," he went on, "But it seems James has been absent for a few days. I thought perhaps Beth might help you, but it seems she's been home with a cold all week."

"And James—why is he out?"

"Can't say. His mother apparently works days, and my secretary has been unable to reach her."

Both of them gone for days. Rather than let my interest show, I just said in a tired voice, "Well, thanks for trying. If you can just give me the boy's address, I'll try my luck at the house."

"Of course. Mrs. Hooper will be happy to look it up for you." Somehow I doubted that. "Anything else I can do to help?"

I stood. "Would you have a picture of James?"

"Certainly." He swiveled his chair around and pulled a leather-bound volume from a low bookshelf. He turned back and spread it open on his desk. "Last year's yearbook," he said. "But he hasn't changed much. A little taller, maybe."

After flipping through several pages, he stabbed his finger down on a small photo, "Here we are."

He rotated the book around as I leaned over to look. A blonde kid with clean-cut looks. A confident, but not cocky expression.

I stuck out a hand. "Thanks for your time, Mr. Duffy."

He pumped my hand. "Happy to help. If you happen to speak to Mrs. Singer, could you ask her to give us a call?"

I promised I would, and he saw me to the door.

* * *

When I got to my car, I found a girl standing beside it. A pretty little dark-eyed brunette, obviously a high school kid. She seemed to be waiting, nervous. She fidgeted with a little charm bracelet and tapped one foot. I gave her a polite nod as I opened the door.

"Excuse me, officer," she blurted at me.

I stopped and turned. "Yes?"

"I just wondered..." She fidgeted some more. "That is, I wanted to ask...is everything okay? With Beth, I mean?"

"Why would you ask?"

She blushed. "Well, it's just...I was in class and ..." She looked around as if she was afraid someone would hear her. There was nobody else in earshot.

She took a deep breath, and then her words gushed out. "The office called Miss Connors about Jimmy Singer and then about Beth, and I started wondering. See, Beth's sister called me and said Beth didn't come home from school Friday and I haven't seen her since and Jimmy hasn't been at school either, and she's my best friend, and I've been kind of worried, and then I heard the police were here asking about them, and I didn't know if maybe something had happened, and..." She stopped to take a breath at last and looked at me, hopeful. "Is Beth all right?"

Mr. Duffy was right about high school campuses. Word traveled. I gave the girl my most reassuring smile. "Let me guess. Your name is Delia."

She blushed again. "Yes, sir. Delia Morgan."

"Well, Delia," I said. "Not to worry. Beth and her sister had a little tiff, and you know how it is. I'm sure she's fine." She sighed with relief. Before she could hit me with a fresh word flurry, I headed her off. "How well do you know James Singer?"

"Oh, not all that well," she said. "He's in my math class, and we had the same history class last year. But he and Beth..." She looked around again. "She doesn't want her sister to know, but I guess it's all right if I tell you." She lowered her voice as though she still thought she might be overheard. "Is that what they fought about? About Beth and Jimmy?"

"Something like that," I said. "Tell me about Beth and Jimmy."

"Well, they're in love." She smiled happily. "And Jimmy's very sweet—Beth says so, anyway. But she didn't think her sister would approve. Her sister is kind of bossy and overprotective. Beth was waiting to turn eighteen so she could do what she wants, and she said they'd have all the money they needed to... See, Beth's Uncle Griffin—well, that's what she calls him—promised he was going to leave her a lot of money in his will, and Beth thought that if she asked him now, maybe...you know."

Good luck with that, I thought. "Did she ask him?"

She shook her head. "She said they've sort of lost touch lately. But she was just sure that he'd help them out. Oh, I hope she hasn't done anything stupid."

I hoped that, too, but didn't say so. "I'm sure Beth's okay," I said again. "But thanks for talking with me, Delia,"

"You won't tell Beth I've told you all this, will you? I wouldn't want her to think...you know?"

"Scout's honor," I said. I threw in the finger sign for good measure. "And it's best if *you* don't tell anyone we've had this talk, either. At least for now, okay?"

She brightened. "I won't, sir. I promise." People *love* to be part of a secret. I got in and started the car, and she gave me a furtive little wave as I drove away.

Chapter Seven

The address the secretary had given me was no more than ten minutes away from the high school. It belonged to a tiny clapboard house in sore need of a paint job and a little sprucing up of the flower beds. The school's secretary had said only James and his mother lived there—she didn't know of a father.

I got no answer at the door. After knocking three times, I gave it up and walked around back. It didn't look like a neighborhood where the neighbors were too watchful, so I wasn't worried. I went in through a kitchen door—the lock was kid stuff.

The place was clean enough, if not elegant. There were two bedrooms, and it was easy to see whose was whose. James's had two school trophies on a small shelf under an L.A. Angels pennant, a pitcher's glove hanging on the bedpost, and a couple of bats sticking out under the bed. A little footlocker-type trunk under the bed held typical kids' stuff—baseball cards, Little League uniform, comic books, a Boy Scout canteen. The bed itself was neatly made up. A school picture of Beth Chase was tacked up over the schoolboy desk. If Beth was hiding the relationship, James Singer wasn't.

In the closet, I found a red and white letterman's jacket among empty hangers, and a pair of cracked and scuffed baseball cleats, but no other shoes. The dresser drawers were nearly empty of socks and underwear.

I didn't come across anything more helpful, so I locked the place back up and headed toward my car. When I was halfway down the driveway, I saw a tired-looking woman approaching the house carrying a huge cloth purse. She stopped dead when she saw me.

I gave her the Nate Ross smile. "Mrs. Singer?"

She clutched the bag tighter and angled her body a little, like she may bolt. "I'm Muriel Singer. What is it?"

I showed her the juice badge. "I just need to ask you a couple of questions if you don't mind."

She looked me up and down for a few seconds. "Do you mind if we talk inside? I've been on my feet all day."

I followed her into the house and sat on the faded sofa while she made herself comfortable in a rocker. She was mid-forties, had probably been good-looking before care and worry had worn her down. She had the same steady gaze as her son. She leveled it on me.

"What's this about?"

"It's about your son."

She blew out an exasperated breath. "What's he done now?"

"For starters, he hasn't been in school for days. But that's not why I'm here."

At the word *school,* I saw a flicker in her eyes—a brief, foxy expression that was there and then wasn't.

She made a helpless gesture. "Jimmy's eighteen now. I can nag him about going to school, but I can't force him. But if you're not here about school, what do you need?"

I gave her the same bunk about the boy witnessing a crime. I wasn't confident she bought it. She claimed not to know where he was at the moment, but said that he's been home every day when she left the house for work and when she came back again. I wasn't sure I bought *that.*

"I don't usually get home much before dark," she went on. "I'm only home early today because the family I work for went out of town." She flashed a weary smile. "I can get twice the work done without them around."

I smiled. "I can imagine." I stood and stepped toward the door. "Thanks for your time, Mrs. Singer. The school would appreciate a call from you."

She nodded. "What about you? When Jimmy comes home, should I have him call you, or...?"

I couldn't give her my business card. "I'll try and catch him here another time," I said. "Good afternoon, ma'am."

As I was getting in my car, I looked back and saw her peeking at me through the blinds.

* * *

Dusty had a full house by the time I got back to the Buscadero. I had some thinking to do, and his cowboy patrons tended to be noisier than even the typical bar crowd, so I collected my dog and headed for the office and a quiet dinner at Gus's before I knocked off for the night. At the office, I phoned Audrey Chase's number. She had already turned in, but Mrs. Borne said there was still no word.

Chapter Eight

Next morning, I got an early start. Before the sun was fully up, I'd parked half a block from the Singer house. When it was just breaking over the hills, Mrs. Singer came out carrying the same big cloth purse. I thought briefly about following her, thinking she might lead me to Jimmy, but since she was dressed for work, I just sat and watched as she headed up the block toward the streetcar stop.

I have very little patience for stake-out work. After an hour, I was debating calling this one off. I was anxious to check in with Audrey Chase, but decided I'd stick it out for another half hour. It was warm in the car, and I had Monte with me. I leaned over to roll down the window on his side a bit, to let some cool air in and dog breath out. When I sat up straight, I glanced in the side mirror and spotted a young man coming up the sidewalk on the other side of the street.

He was still some distance away, walking from the direction of the streetcar stop. He had the morning sun behind him, so I couldn't make his face out with the glare, but I thought there was something furtive about his walk. When he got half a block closer and passed under the shadow of a tree, I recognized the face from his school yearbook.

"Good morning, Jimmy," I said under my breath.

He ambled up the street, looking watchful, and headed straight to his house. I was tempted to pounce on him then and there, but was also curious to see if anyone might show up to meet him. He wasn't inside for five minutes before he came out again wearing his letterman's jacket. He walked back in the direction he'd come from, and when he covered enough distance, I made a U-turn to follow him.

At first, I thought maybe he was heading off to school, but the car he boarded was going the opposite way. As it left the stop, I fell in behind it.

I had little trouble following the red car east as far as Santa Monica Blvd at Virgil. There, the kid switched to a yellow L.A. Railway car heading south. The going got somewhat trickier as the morning traffic became heavier, but I managed to keep the car in sight. I followed it as it jogged over to Hoover, then continued down Temple.

At the car stop near Echo Park, Jimmy stepped off the car and walked south for two blocks, where he went up the steps of a little rundown two-story hotel. The kind of place where you paid up front and the management, such as it was, didn't care what name you put in the register.

I considered waiting the kid out, but since I had no idea where he'd gone once he went inside and didn't know if there was a back way out, I left off that idea. I found a spot on the same side of the street and parked. I didn't like leaving Monte in the car, so I took him along but skipped the leash.

We went into the small, dingy lobby together. The clerk behind the desk looked ninety if he was a day. A little bald-domed guy with hair sprouting out of both ears, he peered at me through a pair of lenses thick as glass ashtrays. I doubt he could see well enough to know whether I was a guest or not. If he could see that I had a big dog with me, or if he cared, he didn't react.

"Morning, Pop." I wasn't going to bother checking the register. I just gave him a wave as we walked toward what looked like the only stairway—there was no elevator. He nodded and flashed me a half-toothless smile and still said nothing about Monte.

Down a short hallway, I saw two doors with brass numbers, one on either side. I listened briefly at each one but didn't hear a sound from either.

I went up the stairs with Monte at my heels. On the upper floor, I found there were four rooms, two at either end with the stairway down the middle. Fifty-fifty odds. I went to the left and listened at the door to one room, then the other. Not a peep. As I was turning from the second room, one of the doors at the other end opened, and James Singer came bursting out. Something was wrong—I could see it in his face. He noticed me, froze for a second, and his look changed to panic. Before I could move or speak, he was barreling down the stairway.

I went after him, taking the stairs three at a time. By the time I hit the lobby, he was out the double doors and halfway down the steps. Through the lobby's big plate glass window, I saw him hit the sidewalk, hook to the right, and disappear. I pushed through the doors and ignored the six steps, angling through the ice plant to slip and slide down the four-foot embankment to the sidewalk. A narrow alley ran between the hotel and a cut-rate furniture store next door. I heard the clatter of running footsteps and turned up the alley to see the kid maybe twenty-five yards away, his head down and his arms pumping. I couldn't speak for his fastball, but he had to be one hell of a base runner. I'm no Jim Thorpe, and I was figuring there was no way I was going to catch up to this guy, when a blur of movement shot past my legs, and I watched Monte rocketing toward him, so quick his paws hardly seemed to touch the pavement.

The kid looked over his shoulder and gave a little cry of terror when he saw the big dog bearing down on him. He tried to put a little more speed into his step, but it was no use. Monte ate up the distance in seconds, and I started to call him off, thinking he was about to launch one of his flying tackles. I didn't want the kid hurt. At least not before I had a chance to talk to him.

But the mutt surprised us both. He flew past the kid just like he had me, ran another ten yards, and then made a dead stop and pivoted around. He planted his feet in the middle of the alley, bared his fangs, and cut loose with a bloodthirsty snarl. The fur on his neck and shoulders stood out like daggers. He looked like Cerberus at the gates of Hell, and Jimmy laid on the brakes. He made a lunge as if to run back my way, but decided against it. His shoulders sagged, and he stood panting and looking at me with a mixture of fear and defiance on his face.

"Where is she?" he gasped out between breaths when I closed the gap.

I don't know what I'd expected him to say, but it wasn't that. I was fighting for air myself and just managed to get out, "What?"

"Beth," he whined. "What did you do with her?"

"Me?" I started toward him, closing the distance between us. "I came here looking for her, Jimmy."

He gave me the dog eye. "Who are you, mister?"

Monte had stood down by this point. He trotted over to me, tail wagging, and sat down by my feet. He gave me a canine grin, and I could see he was pretty pleased with himself. I gave him a quick pat.

Jimmy looked at him, then at me, and flicked a glance over my shoulder back toward the street. "Don't get any ideas, kid," I warned him. "He's just getting warmed up." I took a step closer. "My name's Nate Ross. I'm a private investigator. Beth's sister hired me to find her."

He eyed me for a long while. I tried to get a read on him. He might have been deciding whether he believed me, or he might have been working out what bullshit story he was going to tell me. Maybe both. Or maybe he was making up his mind to trust me. I couldn't be sure which.

I took out my wallet and showed him my license. It seemed to satisfy him. "They took her," he said at last.

"Who did?"

He shook his head. "I don't know."

"Okay," I said. I hiked a thumb toward the hotel. "That your room up there?" He nodded. "Why don't we go up and have a look, and you can tell me what's going on."

He looked at me for a few seconds more. "Okay."

We walked side by side back down the alley with Monte trailing behind. I studied the kid out of the corner of my eye as we walked. He was a tall, athletic youngster, built for running. "No more little powders, okay?" I said.

"Huh?"

"Don't go running off on me again."

He gave me a weak grin. "I won't."

* * *

The old desk clerk flashed us the same gummy smile as we walked past him and went up the stairs.

The room was in enough disarray that I could see right off there'd been a struggle. Nothing too violent. The bed was made, but the spread and pillows were rumpled, and an open book lay face down on top. I picked it up—more poetry.

"So how long have you two been holed up here?" I asked him.

"Just since yesterday."

"And before that?"

"Las Vegas." He held up his left hand to show me a cheap gold band I hadn't noticed before. "We got married, day before yesterday."

I held in a laugh. "Of course you did." I pulled the chair over, straddled it, and waved him to the bed. He sat. Monte settled down on a throw rug near the door.

"Why don't you tell me the whole thing?"

"We've been planning for a while," he said. "But Beth wasn't of age yet, and she was sure her sister wouldn't give her the okay. She's Beth's legal guardian."

"Whose idea was the phony kidnap angle?"

"I don't know." He shot me a guilty, up-from-under look. "Mine, I guess." He spread his hands in defense. "We needed money for train tickets, hotel, and license, and whatnot. Her sister's rich, and they were kind of on the outs, anyway. We didn't see the harm."

"Did you think her sister was just going to sit on her hands?"

"We told her Beth would be back Monday. In the note, I mean. That was the plan. We were going to go up there together and lay it all out. Beth figured she'd be mad, but what could she do about it? It would be a done deal."

"Why didn't you?"

"Beth got cold feet. You know how girls are—she started crying, talking about how she couldn't face her sister, how disappointed she would be, stuff like that. I tried to tell her it would all work out all right. We were going to go see her tomorrow. But now..." He looked around the room with despair.

"And now," I prompted, "What's up?"

He gave his head a violent shake. "I don't know, Mr. Ross. I left her here

49

while I went home to pick up a couple of things. When I got back, she was gone, and…" He waved a hand around the room. "This."

"So you think somebody snatched her for real?"

He glared at me like I was the king of fools. "Does it look like leaving was her idea? Her clothes are gone, but her other stuff is still here." He leaned over and put his head in his hands. "Shit! What am I going to do now?"

I gave him a moment to simmer down. "Well, sonny," I said. "I'm going to do what I was paid to do. I'm going to find her. As for you, I think you better come with me, and we'll go see big sister, let her know how things stand."

He looked up at me. "What about the police?"

"She took your note seriously. There are no cops in the mix yet, just me. I think that's the least of your worries, anyhow."

"Yeah, I guess," he said. He sat up, took a deep breath, "Okay, let's go."

Chapter Nine

I stood out in the shade of the porte-cochere and burned a cigar while they talked things over. I was confident Audrey wouldn't murder the kid, but whatever she had to say to him wasn't for my ears. From the sounds I could catch, she was saying plenty. I couldn't make out what, but I could tell she was hitting Jimmy with some pretty hard words. I didn't have much sympathy. He's earned every one of them—the two young idiots had put the poor woman through hell.

"Welcome to the grown-up world, Jimmy," I said to myself. "Trust me, kid, it doesn't get any easier from here."

While I smoked and thought over this new development and thanked my lucky stars I wasn't in Jimmy Singer's shoes, I saw the big blue Packard coming up the long driveway. It coasted to a smooth stop under the canopy, and Spencer stepped out. As he came around the car, he touched his cap.

"Mr. Ross." He started to say more, but noticed the big dog lying next to me. "He truly is a magnificent animal."

"He likes to think so."

Spencer caught the muffled hubbub from inside the house. His shaggy brows went up a fraction. "Is Miss Chase quite all right, sir?" He moved a half step toward the house, and I flashed the palm like a traffic copper.

"She's just letting off some necessary steam, Spencer. Best you and I stay out here. That much steam could cook a guy like a lobster." I didn't see any harm in telling him—he was going to hear soon enough, so I filled him in. He listened with his usual impassive face.

When I'd laid the whole story out, he asked, "And what is to be done now, sir?"

I offered him a cigar, which he politely declined. I took a long draw on my own, tried to blow a smoke ring or two. Too much breeze.

"Unfortunately," I said, "we're pretty much back at the starting gate. We haven't got a clue who's got the girl—the kid claims to be as much in the dark as we are. So until we get some sort of demand..." I shrugged.

"Maddening, sir. Intolerable."

"Tell me, pal."

Just then, the door opened, and Jimmy came out. Mrs. Borne was close behind him, her mouth a straight, angry line. She gave him the evil eye for a second or two, then glanced at me.

"Miss Chase would like to speak to you, Mr. Ross."

I hesitated, not sure what to do with my half-smoked cigar. Mrs. Borne stepped toward me and held out a hand. I gave her the cigar, and she looked at it with distaste, then walked toward the end of the house and disappeared around the corner. I wondered what she intended to do with it. Bury it among the begonias, maybe. I was reasonably sure she didn't plan to finish it.

All this time, Jimmy stood silent, hands in his pockets and staring at his shoes. Red spots burned in both his cheeks. Overall, he didn't look as whittled down as I had expected.

Spencer regarded the kid with a steelier expression than I'd have thought him capable of. "Shall I drive this young man home, sir?" he asked in a tight voice.

"No, I'll take care of that," I answered. "We still have some talking to do. Can I leave these two in your charge for now?"

"Very good, sir."

"Stay put, boy," I told Monte. "You, too," I said to the kid. He nodded without looking up.

* * *

Audrey was still flushed when I met her in the living room. She had looked pretty stricken when I first told her the news, but giving young Jimmy what-for seemed to have brought some of her strength back.

We talked things over quickly. She was still leery of bringing in the cops. I repeated what I had told Spencer—that there wasn't much we could do until we heard from whoever had Beth and knew what their intentions were.

She assured me that she was all right and told me that she'd be in touch the second she heard anything. As I started to leave, she grabbed my hand in both of hers.

"Promise me, Nate. Promise me she's all right, that we'll get her back safe."

I knew I was a fool to make her a promise. I also knew I'd be a fool to tell her so. I looked deep into her pleading eyes and put a hand on her shoulder.

"I promise." She relaxed her grip, and I turned to go. Now I had no choice.

"You're an idiot, Nathaniel," I muttered to myself as I went out the front door.

* * *

Jimmy just sat and stared out the window as we made our way down the driveway and out through the front gate. Monte slept quietly in the back seat. Half a mile down the private road, I decided to break the silence.

"How'd it go, kid?" He looked at me and scoffed, as though the answer should be obvious. "That good, huh?"

He looked out the window again. "Well, she's not planning to sic any lawyers on me. I guess that's something." He was trying to sound hard, but his voice choked a little. "But what difference does that make if we can't get Beth back?"

He sounded pitiful, but I didn't have time or inclination to spend any sympathy. "You listen to me, Jimmy, and listen tight. In the first place, there is no *we*. You've caused enough trouble already—I'm dealing you out." He looked back at me and opened his mouth to protest, but I shut him down. "You can like that or not, but you're done. I've got a job to do, and I can't do it if I'm tripping over some snot-nosed kid with a bad dose of puppy love."

That bristled him, and he started to open his trap again. I stomped the brake, and we fishtailed a bit and ground to a stop. "You say one word, and I shit you not, I'll toss you out on your ass, and you can leg it home. Get me?"

He started to answer, but checked himself and nodded.

"That's more like it," I growled. I started us down the long, curving road again. "And in the second place," I said, "there's a small chance whoever has your girl is going to contact you instead of her sister. Not likely, but I'm sure by now they know the two of you are hitched. So you are going to plant your little candy ass at home with mommy and wait for a note, phone call, or whatever." I fished a business card from my pocket and handed it across. I'd already written my home number and the Buscadero number on the back. "You get anything like that—anything—you call me right away and sit tight. This is not something I'm going to argue with you about. Got that?"

"Got it." It was barely a whisper.

"Besides," I said. "I'm sure you and your mother have some things to talk about."

"She knows already." He caught my look. "Not about the note or the money or any of that. But she knew where we were going."

I had to laugh. "Why should I even be surprised?"

I steered through a hairpin turn, and when the road straightened out, I noticed a plume of dust rising far back up the road we'd just traveled. Ahead of it, I caught sight of the long, blue limousine barreling our way. The sound of a madly tooting horn echoed through the canyon.

"What the hell?" Fifty yards ahead was a wide turnout up against the canyon wall. I pulled in and stopped, and twenty seconds later Spencer came around the bend, down the road, and steered in behind us. I met him at the door as he started to get out.

"What's the rush, pal?" I asked, fanning away the swirling dust.

Spencer was red-faced and breathless. "Miss Chase needs you right away, sir. She's received a telephone call."

Chapter Ten

"It's much the same as the note," Audrey explained. She shot a murderous glance at Jimmy. I'd planned to have Spencer drive him home while I returned to the estate, but the kid had insisted, pointing out that the kidnappers obviously weren't going to be contacting him now. It was no time to debate, and for better or worse, he *was* the girl's husband. So here we were.

"They're asking for twenty thousand dollars." Audrey's voice was shaky with emotion. "They let me speak with Beth briefly. She says she hasn't been harmed, but…" She broke out sobbing, and I sent Mrs. Borne for a glass of water. When Audrey had had a sip or two and was calmer, she went on. She read from a pad of paper she'd written the instructions down on. I could see that the paper was tear-stained and the writing a little smeared.

"The money's to be in fifty and hundred-dollar bills, unmarked, and left in the…" She paused and drew in a deep breath. "In the toilet tank of the men's room at the Moondance Club on Pico. I told them I would need some time to get that much currency, so we're to deliver the money tomorrow night by nine o'clock. They said to place the money there and then leave the area, that they'll be watching. They warned that if I contacted the police, that … that…" She gasped for air, and then her whole body shook with a violent fit of weeping. She seemed about to take another nosedive. I took a seat beside her on the sofa and put an arm around her shoulders to steady her. I laid my hand on hers.

"Easy, kid. Easy." She slowed down to gentle sobbing, then gulped more air and turned frightened eyes on me.

"They said that if I tried any 'nonsense' that they would send Beth back to me a piece at a time. Oh, God!" She clapped both hands over her mouth and started a muffled wailing.

Jimmy had stood quiet all this time, a strained look on his face. "What are we going to do?" he yelped.

"I already told you what *you're* going to do," I said. "That doesn't change."

He gave me a defiant look but didn't say anything more. Audrey left off crying and rocked forward, hands between her knees, and stared across the room at nothing in particular.

"Is the money going to be a problem?" She didn't answer me. "Audrey." Her head turned slowly, and she looked at me as though she'd forgotten I was there. "Can you get that much cash together that quick?"

"Yes." Her eyes focused, and she seemed to come back to herself. "Yes, I can go to the bank first thing tomorrow."

"Okay, then you do that. Fifties and hundreds, just like they said."

She nodded. "And what are you going to do?"

"I need to get going. I've got some arrangements to make."

Chapter Eleven

Some days it doesn't pay to get out of bed. Some days, I wished I'd listened to my mother and become an architect. I rolled out of the sack before sunup, showered, shaved, and ate a quick toast and eggs breakfast. It was going to be a busy day, and I needed an early start. Monte had the sulks when he realized I was leaving him at home. "Come on, pal," I said to him. "After yesterday, you deserve a day off." I ruffled the fur on his shoulders. "Maybe I'll take you to the Buscadero for a hamburger later, okay?" It didn't seem to satisfy him. He tracked me with baleful eyes as I went out the door.

At the office, I rang the Buscadero and was surprised when Pooter answered. He explained that the shoot he was on had wrapped early, so he was back on the job at the bar. That was welcome news—I was counting on his partner. He told me that Dusty was out picking up supplies, but promised to have him call as soon as he got back.

Not five seconds after I hung up, the phone rang. I grabbed up the receiver. "Morning, Dusty."

"Some pal you are." The angry feminine voice was definitely not my cowboy cohort.

"Aggie," I said. "What makes you so chipper this early in the morning?"

Aggie Underwood was a city desk reporter for the Herald-Express. When it came to sniffing out anything newsworthy, she had the nose of a bloodhound and the tenacity of a bulldog. And if you got on her bad side, she had the temperament of a chihuahua.

"I'll *chipper* you, you bum. A story like this, and you didn't even think to call me? After all the favors I've done you…"

"What the hell are you talking about, Ag?" I asked the question, hoping she didn't mean what I was thinking.

"You're telling me you haven't seen the morning edition?"

"No, I just got in. Hold on." The newspaper had been lying next to the door when I opened up, but I'd been in too much of a hurry to bother with it. I fetched it, not all that sure I wanted to know.

As I dropped back into my chair, I spread it on the desk in front of me. "Oh, shit." So much for hope.

HOLLYWOOD STAR'S SISTER KIDNAPPED, read the big bold headline above photos of both Audrey and Beth Chase. What there was of the story was accurate. It made no mention of Jimmy and Beth's little scheme, only said that the recently married sister had been abducted from the Echo Park hotel where she had been staying. Police had not been notified due to threats from the kidnappers, and they currently had no leads.

"Dandy," I said to myself. So, Aggie had gone to the cops with questions concerning a big-time kidnapping they knew nothing about, and now on page one, they looked like chumps. They were bound to love that.

I was wondering how it could be any worse when I read the next paragraph: *Miss Chase has hired Nate Ross, a Los Angeles private detective, to investigate the matter.* As if that wasn't bad enough, it went on to say, *Ross recently discovered the body of veteran actor Griffin Glenn, former husband of Audrey Chase, at Glenn's home near Bunker Hill. Police suspect foul play, but could not confirm at this point whether his death has any connection to Elizabeth Chase's kidnapping.*

"You still there, Nate?"

"I'm here." I dropped the paper and rubbed my eyes. I felt a sudden headache blossoming behind them. "Jesus, Aggie, you couldn't have talked to me first?"

"I tried, kid. I called you twice, but my editor was in a lather, worried that the *Times* would beat us out. So I had to go with what I had."

"Where did you get this story in the first place?"

"Anonymous call to the front desk."

"And how did you confirm it?"

"How do you think? The lady herself. I hotfooted it up to Audrey Chase's not-so-humble abode and spoke to her in person."

"And she admitted it?"

"You know how persuasive I can be. Plus, I told her you and I were old pals."

"Oh, peachy. Wait…" I tightened my grip on the phone. "You already knew I was on the case when you went out there?"

"The caller said you were."

That bothered me. The kidnap news could have leaked out several ways, but only a handful of people knew I was involved. And if Aggie hadn't gotten it from Audrey Chase…

The story had no details about the phone call or the ransom demand. At least Audrey hadn't told Aggie everything.

"Listen, Ag," I gotta go. "Lots to do today." I fingered the paper. "Even more now."

"Hold on. You're not even going to give me a comment?"

"Are you nuts?" I felt bad as soon as I said it. Aggie was a good egg and a friend, and she just had a job to do, same as me. I softened my tone. "Look, Aggie, I'll tell you all I can when I can. Still pals?"

"We'll see." She still had a grouch on, but I thought I could hear a faint smile creeping in. "You be careful."

I hung up and grabbed my hat. I was halfway to the door when the phone rang again. It could have been Dusty, but I had a suspicion I knew just who was calling. I decided to ignore it and to go over and see Dusty, so I locked the door and headed toward the stairs. I was halfway down when the outer door opened, and I saw I was wrong when the man himself came through it. Queenan. I'd been just thirty seconds from a clean getaway.

"Morning, Cap." I tried not to overdo the cheer. He wasn't having it anyway. The good mood from the other day was gone—he had murder in his eyes. I noticed a tightly rolled newspaper in his fist.

"Back up them stairs, you," he growled. He shook the newspaper at me like a nightstick. "You and me got some things to discuss."

Upstairs, I unlocked the door, and he followed me in with a glance around.

"Where's White Fang at?" He and Monte weren't always on the best of terms.

"Left him at the house."

"Yeah? Too bad for you. You could use the protection." He grunted down into a chair and laid the rolled-up paper on the desk. He took his time trimming and lighting a cigar while he waited for me to take my seat behind the desk. Once I had, he stabbed the cigar into the corner of his mouth, unrolled the newspaper, and tossed it in front of me. "You want to tell me about this?"

I held up my own newspaper. "I've seen it."

"Oh, you've seen it? I'm glad as all hell to hear that. Now, how about you explain it to me?"

"What part of it?"

"The part where you just happen to stumble across a murder the other day, a murder of a rummy actor who's connected to the victim in this snatch caper." He nailed the paper to the desk with a stubby finger. "The part where you held out on me that you were workin' the biggest kidnap case since Lucky Lindy."

I held my hands up in defense. "First of all, Cap, when I talked to you at Glenn's, I wasn't convinced it *was* a kidnapping, and as it turns out, it wasn't then."

He nearly spit out his cigar. "Come again?"

I laid the whole story out for him—Beth and Jimmy's harebrained plan to elope, and how their fake kidnapping had turned into the real thing.

He waved the cigar in the air and squinted at me. "And what makes you think this Singer punk's not just feeding you a line of shit?"

"He wasn't putting on any show. The kid was surprised, upset. The marriage story's the goods—I saw the license. Anyway, he was with me when Audrey Chase got the call."

"Yeah, okay. Still, if you thought the first caper was the bunk, you coulda clued me in."

"I wasn't sure if it was or it wasn't, Cap. Anyway, Miss Chase was taking it seriously, and the note threatened curtains for the sister if the cops got involved."

"Well, we're sure as hell involved now."

"I guess you are," I said. "But why you? You're Homicide."

"Because of the chance that the Griffin Glenn thing's connected to this caper."

"I don't see how, since he was bumped before she was taken."

"There's that. But also, you know as well as I do that a kidnapping can turn into a homicide. Especially," he said, picking up the newspaper, "when exactly what the kidnapper said better not happen happens."

He seemed to have simmered down, and I was anxious to get going, so I asked, "Are we done here for now?"

"Done?" He yanked the cigar from his mouth and dropped an inch of ash in his lap. He brushed it away with a muttered curse. "We ain't done, Ross. We're just gettin' started."

"What's that mean?"

He gave a snort of laughter and fixed me with a malignant smile. "Oh, I get it. You were thinkin' all I came here for was to read you the riot act."

"All right, I'll bite. Why *are* you here?"

"The Chief put me on this case himself. Not the Chief of Detectives—*the Chief*." He pointed at the newspaper. "And since L.A.'s crack private eye has been working it already—buddy boy, he says you and me are now partners."

Chapter Twelve

Dusty, who never showed surprise at anything, looked dumbstruck when Queenan and I walked in together. As he recovered, he stretched a hand across the bar to shake hands with Queenan. "Hello, Captain."

"Vanner."

Dusty looked at us each in turn with curiosity. "Never fancied I'd see the two of you coming in here like *buenos amigos*."

"That'll be the day," Queenan said. The place was empty but for three old timers who sat around a table near the jukebox. Queenan gave them a bored once-over.

"Pooter said you called," Dusty said, half as a statement, half as a question.

"Yeah. Can you get him to watch the place while we talk in the office?"

"You bet." He gave us another questioning look, then went to the swinging door that led into the kitchen. "Hey, Pooter. Watch the front a spell. I'll be in the back."

I heard a clatter of dishes from the kitchen, but no answer. Dusty called out again, "Pooter!"

"I heard you, I heard you," came the muffled reply.

"Cranky old bastard," Dusty muttered. He waved us to follow.

In the office, I ran down the whole story for Dusty, right up to my talk with Queenan. He couldn't suppress a huge grin.

"The two of you in harness together," he said with a laugh. "Now that's a pair to draw to. I'd have bet my eye teeth I'd never live to see *this* day."

"You and me both, Tex," Queenan grumbled.

"So I'm guessing you boys are here because you could use an extra hand," Dusty said.

"We could," I answered. "The drop's tonight, and we need to keep a close eye on it the best we can from inside the club. I'm no good, since the numbskull who did the piece in this morning's *Times* included my picture. These guys, whoever they are, can probably spot a copper a mile off, so that leaves Queenan and his boys out."

We spent another half hour hashing out a plan and agreed to meet at my office at 5:00.

* * *

Queenan and I drove out to Audrey Chase's estate in his department bus. We didn't talk much, which was fine by me. I was no happier about this partnership deal than he was.

He was unusually quiet and polite when I introduced him to Audrey Chase. I could see that even the crusty old copper wasn't immune to her charms. Maybe a little star-struck, too. For her part, she was courteous to him but seemed a little cold and stiff toward me.

Once we were seated in the living room and Queenan had declined the offer of coffee, Audrey abruptly got to her feet. "Captain Queenan," she said, "Would you mind at all if I spoke privately with Mr. Ross for a moment? It's a personal matter—I hope you understand."

"Sure thing," Queenan said. He started to rise.

"No, please, make yourself comfortable," Audrey told him. "We can step out into the garden."

Queenan sat back. He watched me closely as I followed Audrey out through the French windows.

Fifty feet down the flagstone path, she turned to face me. "Tell me it wasn't you, Nate."

"What are you talking about?"

"The newspaper. Tell me you didn't tell the press Beth had been kidnapped."

"Are you serious? Of course I didn't. I would never—

"How did they know?" Her voice was sharp, accusatory, and her eyes were alert and searching.

"Aggie Underwood said they got a call. Anonymous."

"She told me that as well," Audrey said. "Then she brought up your name."

"We're old friends," I told her. "But not friends enough that I'd sell out a client for a little cheap publicity. Believe me, Audrey. I don't play those games. Aggie told me the caller gave them my name." She continued to study my face.

"Look, if I'd told the press, they'd have the whole story. The pieces in the paper don't mention any details about Jimmy and Beth, or the phone call, or how much ransom, or the drop. If they'd had that information, trust me, they'd have published it. But they don't have it because I didn't give it to them. And you didn't give it to Aggie, which is why I haven't asked if it was *you* who tipped them."

That shook her a little, and I saw doubt come into her eyes.

"Let's not forget," I reminded her, "You got frosty with me when you thought I was implying that *you* had cooked this up for publicity."

She looked at me a moment more, then her eyes dropped. "You're right. You are absolutely right." She brought her eyes back up. "But who could have called them?"

I gave an exaggerated look around the grounds. "I can think of a couple of possibilities."

"Oh, no," she said, "Spencer and Mrs. Borne couldn't, wouldn't. I trust them completely. They've…kept other secrets." She gave me a meaningful look.

"Beth?" I asked. She nodded. "They both know?"

She nodded again. "And believe me, if they were inclined to sell my secrets…"

I thought about it for a moment. "Okay," I said. "In any case, it's out there now, and we can't help that. We've got more important things to talk about. And we should probably go back in—Queenan needs to be in on this part."

We walked back toward the house. She laid a hand on my arm, and we stopped.

"I apologize, Nate. It was foolish of me."

"Not a bit," I said. "You had the right to wonder. No harm done."

Queenan didn't say anything when we came back inside, but I caught him giving me the dog eye once or twice. Audrey had the money ready as ordered. Queenan wrote her a receipt and took charge of the bulky envelope.

We explained our plans for the drop to her, and she listened with an eager and anxious face. She told Queenan that she hoped he wouldn't take offense, but with the ominous warning the kidnappers had given her, she was very worried about having the police involved in the drop.

"I understand your concern, Miss Chase," he said in as soothing a voice as he could muster. "But believe me, it's for the best. I've done this sort of thing before, and I can promise you this is our best chance of identifying the miscreants involved in this crime. We'll get your sister home soon, and with luck, your money as well." He patted the envelope in his coat pocket.

"The money's of little concern, Captain. Just get Beth back to me." She brushed tears away with the heel of a hand. "That's all I care about."

Queenan dipped his chin. "Of course, ma'am."

* * *

Queenan noticed my look as he navigated us down the private road. "What?"

"Nothing. I've just never heard you talk like that before. Didn't know you even spoke the King's English."

"Blah," he spat out. "The world ain't big enough to hold all that you don't know."

"*Miscreants?*"

"Go to hell." He closed one eye and cocked the other at me. "And don't think I didn't see you two getting all kissy-kissy in the garden there."

"Piss up a rope, Cap. She's a client. Period."

He grinned and shook his head. "Don't bullshit a bullshitter, Ross."

I didn't say anything to that. He was just baiting me, and I was in no mood to give him the satisfaction.

"You know," he said after five minutes of silent driving. "We gotta have someone make the drop. Somebody our body snatchers aren't gonna make."

"She used her chauffeur last time, but I'm not sure that's a good idea. Who knows what these mutts might pull? We need somebody a little more crook savvy. I've got a guy in mind."

Chapter Thirteen

Queenan dropped me at the office and left for the station. He had Decker and some of his other boys combing the department's files, looking at all known or suspected kidnap artists. This seemed like a professional job—somebody had evidently been watching Beth and Jimmy pretty closely, had maybe even caught on to what they were up to. Just to cover all bases, Queenan was going to see what, if anything, their files had on Jimmy.

I put a call into Danny Isaac, then went down to Gus's for a quick cup of coffee. Afterward, I swung by home to pick up Monte.

Ten minutes after we got back to the office, Danny Issac came down the hallway. I'd wanted to talk to him early to be sure he'd be available later—I wasn't the only P.I. he did jobs for.

He stiffened when he saw Monte. The big dog trotted over to him with a swishing of his big, bushy tail, and Danny flattened himself against the wall. As Monte sniffed him, Danny gave his head a wary pat. He sighed with relief when Monte went back to his blanket in the corner.

"Why you gotta run around with that monster, Nate?"

"Because he does what he's told," I said. "And he doesn't pull bloomers that end up costing me money."

"Aw, are you still beefing about that?" he whined. "Look, I say again—"

I laughed. "Easy, pal. I'm just ragging you."

He gave me a baleful look. "Okay, so anyway, you said you got another job for me? Somethin' good, I hope—I ain't workin' no more shoplift capers."

"No, this is a gravy job. No running necessary. How's fifty for the easiest night's work you've ever done grab you?"

He licked his lips. "Fifty dollars?"

I threw my pencil at him. I wasn't in the mood for his dumb questions. "No, Florins."

His eyes narrowed in confusion, so I added, "Dollars—what the hell do you think?"

"Just askin'. Jeez, you're touchy," he said as he picked the pencil up from the floor between his feet. "You know, you could put a guy's eye out like that."

"Not me. I trained with a Mexican knife thrower."

He gave me one more baleful look and dropped the pencil on my desk. Just then, the news program I'd been half listening to ended, and I heard a familiar sax and horn intro fade in.

"Turn that up, will you, Danny?"

He reached over a shoulder to turn up the radio, and his face took on a dreamy expression.

"Basie. *The Blues I Like to Hear.*" He turned back to me. "I seen his show live once, you know? In Philly, when I was visitin' my sister."

I didn't say anything to that. I didn't want to encourage any more chatter while the Count was playing. Today had few enough pleasures.

"He's in town, you know. Seen it in the paper."

Though Danny wasn't overly bright, he was a religious reader of the daily newspapers and could usually rattle off even the most insignificant news of the day. And would, whether anyone was interested or not.

Of course I knew. But I should have known silence wasn't going to deter Danny. It only gave him space to fill.

"Is that right?" I tried to sound as uninterested as I could, hoping a neutral response would shut him up, or at least start him on a different topic. It didn't work.

"Sure. You ain't heard?" He straightened in his seat, puffed up a little like he always did when he thought he knew something I didn't. "Him and Jimmy Rushing and the whole gang. Was gonna play at the Palomar, but I guess you heard what happened there."

I gave him a sharp look to see if he was trying to needle me, but his eyes were all innocence. "Yeah, I heard," was all I said. If he didn't know, I wasn't about to go into *that* topic with him.

"So now they're gonna play the Paramount," he went on.

Great. And me with a case on my hands that wasn't likely to leave me any spare time.

I held up a silencing hand as halfway through the song Rushing's heavy baritone came in over the horns. It took a rare set of pipes to do that. I didn't consider myself any sort of connoisseur of music—far from it. But even my tin ear could tell that Count Basie and his orchestra were in a class all their own. As I sat back and let the mellow blues wash over me like a warm breeze, I couldn't help but be a little jealous that an uncivilized little half crook like Danny Isaac had experienced them in person and I hadn't, and probably never would.

Thankfully, Danny kept it buttoned for the rest of the number and let me have my three minutes of bliss. Even Monte seemed to share in it. He'd sat up alert at the first sound of Rush's voice, then settled down with a soft, contented grunt and lay with his eyes half-closed and his feathery tail swaying in near-perfect time with the beat. Who knew the big beast was a blues fan?

The song over and the trance broken, I gave Danny brief details about the job I had for him and told him to be sure and be back by six.

He nodded his understanding and gingerly stood to go, keeping one eye on the half-sleeping dog.

After Danny left, Monte and I went back down to Gus's for a quick bite since we weren't going to have time for dinner later. Back in the office, Monte was napping by the time Dusty showed up at a quarter to five, but he woke up when Queenan arrived ten minutes later and greeted the copper with his usual low growl. Queenan made sure he took the chair that put Dusty between him and the dog.

We wanted to make sure we had plenty of time to get our plans down and to have Dusty in place well before the drop to avoid suspicion. The kidnappers had told Audrey they'd be watching, but we had no idea if they'd be keeping tabs from outside or inside the place. Likely both.

I had told Danny not to show back up until six, not because I didn't trust him, but because his only job was to make the drop and to keep his eyes open. He didn't need to know the whole story.

We bided our time with cigars and watched the clock. Queenan said his detectives had gone through twenty years of files on kidnappings and come up with only a couple of unlikely possibles. Most of the snatch artists the department had jackets on were either dead, doing time at San Quentin or Folsom—with a few at Alcatraz—or had drifted off to terra incognita. They hadn't come across anybody promising.

"How about James Singer, or Audrey's—Miss Chase's—staff? Anything on them?"

Queenan grinned with his eyes at my correction. "We got no records on the Singer kid, juvie or adult. He's only been eighteen for a couple of months."

"And the chauffeur and housekeeper?"

"Decker talked to them both and checked them up. Nada. Both clean as a preacher's sheets. Though the boys had their doubts about this Spencer bird at first. Kind of cagey about givin' them his whole name."

"Which is?"

He gave me a mock serious look. "Sorry, Ross. The boys promised him they'd keep it on the q.t., and you of all people know how important it is to respect a confidence." He jiggled his cigar with his teeth and winked.

I could see it was going to be a long night. Just for a change of subject, I asked, "You boys getting anywhere on the Griffin Glenn thing?"

He looked at Dusty, then shook his head. "What the hell—he's just gonna tell you all this, anyhow." He turned back to me. "It's slow goin', now that we're dealin' with this caper. The print crew took some lifts off the frame of that upstairs door. Not the rummy's, but we haven't made any matches yet."

"I've been meaning to ask you—you guys find a will in the house?"

"No, just some letters between Glenn and his lawyer that mentioned his will. Why?"

I told him about the talk I'd had with Delia Morgan.

He shook his head. "From the looks of it so far, he couldn't have been leavin' the Chase girl much of a boodle. You saw his bank book. And he didn't own the house he was in—rental. Plus, he owed money all over town."

"You talk to the lawyer yet?"

He scoffed. "You know how cooperative these damn shysters are." He looked at Dusty again. "No offense to your son." Dusty waved the comment away, and Queenan turned back to me. "Besides, Glenn owed this guy a stack, too. Decker was gettin' together a warrant for the will, but now with this mess to handle…"

"Will you let me know? About the will?"

"How often do I have to tell you, it's an open case, Ross. And anyway, you was hired to work on gettin' the girl back. Period." He stared at the ceiling and puffed his cigar. "For now, let's just get this business over with." He looked at his watch. "You're sure we can count on this guy?"

"Danny's okay," I said. "He's not winning any scholarships, but we don't need him to do any headwork—just drop the cash and fade. Anyway, he's con wise enough to spot anything—or anyone—that's not on the square."

Queenan didn't look convinced but didn't say so. He looked even less convinced when six o'clock rolled around, and Danny showed up. Danny's not an impressive looking guy. He's only a shade over five-foot-four, and his short, bowed legs and overlong arms, plus a long upper lip and low-set, almost perfectly round ears, give him the appearance of a friendly little chimp.

Queenan didn't try hard to disguise his reservations when Danny shook hands with him and Dusty in turn. Dusty had seen Danny at work a time or two and knew he was capable enough as long as you didn't let him do much of the thinking.

We didn't tell Danny any more than he needed to know, but when I explained his part in the evening's festivities in detail, and Queenan handed over the envelope, Danny flashed us a knowing grin.

"This is about that movie dame, right? That hotcha blonde whose sister got snatched?"

"That's to be kept under the hat, bub," Queenan rumbled. "Not for circulation. Get me?"

"Whatever you say, Fosdick." Naturally, Danny didn't neglect the funny papers in his daily reading.

Queenan's jaw muscles bulged, and I thought he might tear the arms off the chair he sat in. To avoid any bloodshed, I cut in with a quick change of subject.

"Listen, Cap," I said. "I figure we should drive my bucket. These mopes will be on the lookout for a city car or anything that says copper."

"Fine by me," Queenan said in a flat voice, still giving Danny the hard eye.

"There's a parking lot up the block where the three of us can watch from. It's got a view of both the front and side entrance to the place."

"Yeah, okay." He stopped eyeballing Danny and looked at me. "What do you mean us *three*? Vanner's gonna be inside."

"You, me, and Monte."

"Monte?" It hit him, and I thought he might swallow his cigar. "The *dog*? Are you nuts, Ross? I ain't sittin' stakeout with no slobbering dog breathing his stink down my back the whole damn night."

Monte heard his name and sat up, alert and interested. He seemed to understand Queenan's words and fixed him with a hostile stare.

"He might come in handy, Cap," I said. "He can run faster and jump fences better than either one of us can."

"He farts," Queenan grumbled.

"So do you. Don't think I haven't noticed."

"Blah." He waved my words away. "Anyhow, the mutt don't like me."

"So what—you think I do? Trust me, if it comes to it, you'll be glad I brought him along."

"He bites me, I don't guarantee you I won't shoot him."

"He's not going to bite you." I looked over at the big dog. "Are you, boy?"

Monte dropped down and lowered his head onto his paws with a disappointed little whine.

Chapter Fourteen

I was passingly familiar with the Moondance Club. I'd been there on a previous case. "Club" was a little high-hat for the place—it was a glorified barroom not much bigger than the average corner gin mill, with a small dance floor and a stage just large enough for a quartet to play on. Maybe a dozen tables, and no food served.

Dusty had gone into the place at a quarter to seven while Queenan, Danny, Monte, and I parked in the bowling alley lot just up the street. I'd wanted to have Danny come in on his own, but Queenan refused to have him walking around carrying twenty grand in cash. Whether he didn't trust Danny or whether he thought the little guy might get held up, he didn't say, and I didn't argue the point. Danny was none too happy to have to share the back seat with Monte, so I soaped him by offering him an extra ten dollars for his trouble.

Our plan was for Dusty to take a seat that allowed him a view of who came and went to the men's room. He'd order drinks and listen to the band, and to anyone watching would be just another customer out for a cheap night on the town. I persuaded him it would be better if he dressed like a regular Joe and left off his usual cowboy garb. I had to loan him my fedora and a spare coat I kept at the office—the boots we were stuck with. Decked out as he was, if it hadn't been for the wild mustache, which we couldn't do anything about either, I'd have hardly recognized the guy.

For Danny's part, he was to walk into the club at eight sharp, have a beer at the bar, then go into the restroom and stash the money in the toilet tank. We tied the envelope up in an oilcloth pouch to keep it dry. Danny would take note of anybody he thought looked suspicious, but once he'd dropped the cash, he was to head straight out of the club, hail a cab, and beat it. If he'd seen anything or anyone he didn't like the look of, he'd have the cabbie circle back around, drop him off a block or two away, and make his way back to us to clue us in. If he didn't, his job was done for the night.

Once the money was in place, Dusty would monitor the restroom comings and goings. He'd check on the money as often as he could without being obvious, but otherwise, we were depending on his observation skills and gut instinct to spot any pickup men. As long as the money remained, Dusty would stick right up until the place closed at two. We were banking on nobody from the club staff being our boys—only a cluck would pull a caper like this where he was known, and the birds we were dealing with seemed a little too sharp for that.

At ten minutes to eight, Danny said, "Wish me luck, boys," climbed out of the car, and went into the bowling alley. He'd cool his heels there so nobody would spot him going from my car to the club, then come out again a few minutes later, cross the street, and head for the Moondance.

"I sure hope this pans out," Queenan said as we watched Danny in the mirror.

"So do I, Cap. So do I."

Just short of ten minutes later, Danny came back out. He had a slow, casual walk and a way of looking like he was lost in his thoughts, but I knew he was taking in every detail, face, passing car. It was why he was so valuable for shadow jobs.

Once Danny was inside, Queenan and I kept watch on the front of the club. Foot traffic wasn't all that heavy, and we didn't see anyone to raise our antennas. Several people—men mostly—came and left, and nothing much went on.

"Boy," Queenan said after a while, just to fill the dead air, "This is some exciting life you lead, Ross."

"Me? Don't tell me you haven't done your share of this hurry up and wait crap."

"Sure, but when I stake a joint out, I got a two-way radio to keep me company." He aimed a thumb over his shoulder. "All's you got is Rin Tin Tin here."

"He's good company," I said. "Plus, he keeps his trap shut and never gives me the razoo."

"Blah." He fished in his pockets and came out with one of his rank smelling cigars. He set fire to it and spent the next half hour fouling the air in the car. I didn't kick about it. It kept his mouth busy.

I guess Danny nursed his beer for as long as he could. At 8:14 by my watch, he walked out of the club and down the sidewalk the same way he had come. As he ambled along, he took off his hat and smoothed his red hair—our signal that the money was in place. He caught a cab at the corner, and they headed west on Pico and out of sight.

And now the longest part of the night began. We had to be extra alert and take note of everyone who came out of the place. Dusty could only go to the can so often without tipping his mitt. And meantime, anybody might be coming out with the money. I'd brought my camera along and shot snaps of everyone who came out while Queenan watched through binoculars for any familiar faces.

Lucky for us, for every seven or eight who went in, only one came out. For the first few hours, anyway. As midnight closed in, more were coming out than going in, and it got trickier to keep up. Dusty hadn't stepped outside. That was a good sign. It meant that as of his last check, at least, the cash hadn't been touched.

There was a lull just after midnight, and my eyelids were starting to get the droops. I saw Queenan stifling a yawn. Even Monte looked tired and bored.

"Hey, Cap, how about grabbing us a cup of coffee?" I pointed toward the bowling alley. "I'll buy if you fly."

"I look like a waitress to you? How about you buy *and* you fly?"

"Fine." I reached for the door handle. "You can stay here with Monte." The big dog perked up at his name and shoved his huge head over the seat back.

Queenan leaned away. "All right, you take cream and sugar or black?" He held out a big mitt, and I dropped a half dollar into it.

"Black. Nothing for my partner, thanks."

He glowered at me and stomped off toward the bowling alley, mumbling to himself.

He was back in ten minutes and handed me a paper cup without a word. I held out a hand, and he looked at it, then at me.

"Change?"

He ignored me and sipped his coffee. I tried mine—a little gritty, but it tasted better than I expected. It was hot at least.

There'd been no sign of Danny returning, so he evidently hadn't seen anything to concern him. For two more hours, Queenan and I sat mostly in silence. Judging from the exits we saw, I didn't think there could be more than a dozen people left inside the club. Still no sign of Dusty.

At two on the mark, the neon sign flickered off, and over the next few minutes the place emptied out in small clusters of people, few of them able to steer a straight line down the sidewalks. As arranged, Dusty came out last of all, and I watched the manager lock the door behind him.

Dusty pulled the same hat gag Danny had, which told us he was carrying the swag. He walked two blocks east to a corner bus stop, and we picked him up there.

"Nothing'doin' tonight," he said as Monte made room for him in the back. He pulled the envelope from his inside coat pocket and handed it over the seat to Queenan.

"You sure nobody made you?" Queenan asked.

"I'm sure," Dusty said. "Wasn't nobody payin' me any mind, not even the waiter. Hell, I thought I'd have to stand up on my table to get another drink."

"Shit." Queenan tucked the money away in his coat and looked at me. "What do you suppose went wrong?"

"Who knows? You know how crook sense is—maybe they smelled a setup. About all we can do now is to wait for their next move."

"Yeah," he said. "And hope that move ain't makin' good on their threats.

Chapter Fifteen

Next morning, I called Audrey first thing to let her know the pickup didn't go off. I'd have preferred to give her the news in person, but I was expecting Queenan to drop into the office. She was pretty shaken, and I did my best to reassure her that things would be okay. It wasn't easy to convince her since I wasn't sure I believed that myself. I was glad when she told me that on Queenan's orders, Decker and another detective had set a tap on her phone, and that they'd stayed at the house through the night to monitor it.

Queenan hadn't shown up by seven, so I left Monte to mind the office while I had breakfast at Gus's. I was having a third cup of coffee and fending off Benjy's questions about the stories in the papers and the case, when I saw Queenan's car pulling into the gravel lot. I dropped a buck on the table and caught up with the big copper halfway to my building.

I could see from his face that something was up. He skipped his usual barbed greeting, and before I could ask, he said, "She's got another call."

His tone didn't tell me much, and I felt my guts twist into a knot. "Is the girl okay?"

"Yeah, yeah," he said. "They put her on the line for a second, and she sounded all right. Scared, but she says they haven't hurt her. Let's go up to your berth, and I'll fill you in."

Monte shot to his feet as we came in, and I got ready to shush him, but he took one look at Queenan and, instead of growling, sat and thumped his tail on the floor.

Queenan dropped into his customary seat. "What's with your buddy? He get laid this morning or what?"

"No, Cap, I think you've finally made yourself a new pal."

He eyed Monte with suspicion. "Lucky me." He dug out a cigar and put a match to it. "Anyways, the call came in about a half hour ago. Same caller, according to your gal friend."

"She's not my—" I wasn't biting. "What did they say?"

"They want more dough. Thirty grand now. Kind of what I thought—they saw the newspapers, and they told her that since she broke the rules, it was going to cost her. She damn near dropped dead when they said that, so they put little sister on the phone to prove she was all right. They told her they'll give her one more chance to come through, but if things go screwy again, that's it for the girl."

"You got a trace on the call?"

"In the works. Decker's talking to the central exchange, but it takes a little time."

"They give her instructions for another drop?"

"Phone booth in the lobby of a movie house on Vine. The Del Rio." He grinned. "You're familiar with that place, right?"

"Yeah, I know it." I'd worked a job there a few months back. A nothing job that had turned into a real bucket of worms. It ended with the two owners, along with quite a few other people, dead. The place was under new ownership, and I'd been hoping to never hear of it again. So it goes.

"The same kind of deal as before," Queenan said. "They told her to tape the envelope under the seat in the booth and clear out. Nine o'clock again. No cops, no shenanigans, blah, blah, blah. Or else."

"Your boys pick up any clues from listening in? Caller's voice, background noise, anything they said?"

"Nah, nothing except like I said, same voice as the first call."

"Okay, you want to play it the same way? I need to call Danny and Dusty."

"We can forget the leprechaun this time around."

"Look, I know you don't like Danny, but—"

"It ain't that," he said. "He done his job all right, I'll give him that. But the kid wants to make this drop."

"The kid?"

"Singer."

"How does he know—"

"He was at the house when the call came in, Decker said. Checkin' to see what news. Anyway, he figures if they were keepin' tabs on him and the girl, they know the two of them tied the knot. He thinks they're maybe less likely to smell a rat this way."

"What do you think?"

"Kid's got a point, I guess. And kid or not, he *is* the girl's husband now, so how can we tell him to butt out?"

I didn't think too much of Jimmy Singer after the dido he'd pulled, but Queenan was right—the kid was entitled to a say in how we handled this. "Well, we'll need to get him in here, then," I said. "Make sure he understands what he's going to do, and especially what he's *not* going to do. The last thing we need is some hot-headed kid trying to play Sir Galahad."

"As for Vanner," Queenan said, "we can definitely use him again. In fact, I've got a sweet little idea there."

* * *

After Queenan left, I called the Buscadero and filled Dusty in on the new demands.

"All right. Meet at your office at 5:00 again?"

"Yeah. And good news—no square John clothes this time around."

"I can wear my own duds?"

"Hat and all. One other thing—can you twirl a rope?"

"Twirl a rope? You mean throw a lasso?"

"No, I mean *twirl* it. You know fancy tricks and all that."

"Well, I ain't no Will Rogers, but I can spin a flat loop all right. But what the hell...?"

"Tell you at five. Just bring a rope."

Chapter Sixteen

Jimmy Singer showed up at the office at a quarter to six. Queenan and Dusty were already there. The plan we laid out for Jimmy was along the same lines as what we'd done the night before. He would come in on his own, buy a ticket for the 8:15 double feature, and go inside. He'd put the envelope in place, then fall in with the crowd leaving the earlier showings and go home to wait for news.

"Straight home," Queenan told him. "No hangin' around to watch the fun. These people aren't foolin' with us."

"I understand, sir," Jimmy said.

* * *

"I've gotta say," I told Queenan as we watched Dusty doing his bit in front of the Del Rio, "That was some damn slick thinking on your part."

"If that's meant to be a compliment," he said, without taking his eyes from the binoculars, "You could try soundin' a little less surprised."

Queenan had driven by the theater on his way to my office in the morning and noticed that it was currently showing two Westerns—*Frontier Marshal* and the *Oklahoma Kid.* It gave him the idea of having Dusty do rope tricks in full cowboy garb next to the box office. He'd look like he was there to promote the films, and he'd have a clear view of the phone booth in the lobby and be in a position to spot the pickup.

We watched from my Ford parked in a lot next to a steakhouse half a block away. This time around, Queenan hadn't bucked at all about bringing Monte along. The big dog snored softly in the back seat. He liked to conserve his energy.

"Lucky break for us, this dump don't get first-run pictures. They're playin' two oaters that have already been out a while. You seen 'em?"

"Are we going to spend the night making small talk, Cap?"

"Jeez, just tryin' to pass the time," he grumbled. "You gotta be an asshole?"

"Fine." I held up my hands in surrender. "No, I haven't. I don't get out to the movies much. Have you seen them?"

"Yeah, couple of months back. The one with Randolph Scott's pretty good. Lot of shoot-'em-up action."

"How about the other one?" I tried my best to sound interested.

He chuckled. "A Western with Jimmy Cagney? And Bogart? I bet the guy who sold the studio *that* idea is back workin' the mail room." He sat up straight. "Look sharp, pal. There's the kid."

I looked up the street and spotted Jimmy coming up the sidewalk from the direction of Santa Monica Blvd. A couple of people were ahead of him when he reached the box office, and he cast a nervous glance around him as he waited. I was glad to see he didn't do more than glance at Dusty. We'd warned him he'd risk giving Dusty away if he paid too much attention.

Once the kid had his ticket, he went inside. I watched him through my camera. From the angle we were at, I had no view of the telephone booth. There were actually three booths, side by side—the caller had said to place the money in the middle one.

Jimmy had tucked the envelope under his waistband and wore his bulky letterman's jacket to hide the otherwise noticeable bulge. The package was bulkier now with the additional ten grand in hundreds Queenan's guys had gotten from Audrey.

I'd warned the kid to avoid the natural urge to touch the concealed envelope. We couldn't afford to have him fall prey to a stickup artist or a pickpocket. So far, he was heeding my advice and keeping his hands away, but he looked fidgety as he loitered by the snack counter. He kept shifting from one foot to the other and constantly fussed with his cuffs. I couldn't blame him for being nervous—he was just a kid, and there was a lot on the line—but I wished he'd just take care of his errand and get out of our way.

"Come on, Jimmy," I said under my breath. "Quit looking around. Just plant the damn package and beat it out of here."

"Here he goes," Queenan said, tracking with his binoculars. Jimmy walked out of sight toward where I knew the phone booths were.

"It's all up to the cowboy now." Queenan said. I watched Dusty spinning a loop overhead and chatting with a young couple. He looked casual enough but stared past them as they talked. I knew he had his eyes on the phone booth.

Jimmy came out a minute later, and as he hit the sidewalk, he ran a hand through his hair. The money was in place. He stuffed his hands in his jacket pockets and sauntered back down the sidewalk toward Santa Monica to board the streetcar and head home.

Now my attention was all on Dusty, while Queenan continued to scan the movie crowd and passersby for any known hoodlums. We were expecting a wait. It was barely 8:35, the kidnappers had given us until nine o'clock, and the last show wasn't over until 12:20. But not ten minutes later, Dusty quickly turned our way and spun his rope in a horizontal figure eight. It was the signal.

"Shit, Cap, they're early," I said as I hit the starter.

"They must have been watching the kid," he said as we bounced out onto Vine and toward the theater. I braked right in front, and angry drivers honked horns and cursed as Dusty cut across the street and jumped into the back seat with Monte.

Dusty leaned in between me and Queenan. "See that fella in the tan raincoat, gray hat with the black band?" He pointed to a guy walking down the block toward Santa Monica.

Queenan followed Dusty's finger. "You're sure about it?"

"Yep. I seen him come up with the envelope, plain as day. Tucked it inside his coat."

"All right, then," Queenan said. "Let's see where he heads to. Don't get too close, Ross."

The traffic was thick enough that I could keep us three cars back and slow enough that I was in no danger of overtaking the guy. He didn't seem watchful or hurried, but walked with a casual stride and continued south on Vine just as the kid had done.

At Santa Monica, I pulled to the curb, and we watched our boy board the east-bound P.E. car. I followed the car for several blocks and pulled over again as it stopped at Western. A few passengers left the car, but not our pickup man. The car stopped again at Virgil, and this time he got off. He waited at the stop for several minutes, standing off by himself, and when the downtown car came along and stopped, he climbed aboard. I followed this car through a couple more stops, but the guy stayed put. It hit me that this was the same route I'd followed Jimmy Singer down to his hotel, and I briefly wondered if there was some connection. But as we continued on past Echo Park, our bird still hadn't left the car.

Not until we'd stopped near Temple and Figueroa did we see the man again. Except that I thought I was seeing double.

"What the hell's this?" Queenan barked. Two men stepped off the car, both wearing tan raincoats and gray fedoras with black ribbon bands. Same height, same build. Dusty had been watching the pickup guy's hands, not his face, and Queenan and I had only seen him from behind, so we had no idea which of the two was our quarry.

The two men didn't acknowledge each other, but walked down the sidewalk on Figueroa, where one turned east and the other west.

We both looked at Dusty. He spread his hands. "Sorry, fellas, I wish I could tell you. Could be either of 'em."

"Son of a bitch." Queenan said. "We're gonna have to split up then, follow 'em both. You take east, Vanner. Ross, and I will take west." He wrote down something in his notebook, tore out the page, and gave it to Dusty. "Here's the phone number for the Chase dame's chateau. Your guy goes to ground, call Decker there and tell him where you are."

Dusty nodded, got out, and started walking east. Queenan cracked his own door open, looked at me. "Let's take it on the leg from here. I doubt he's going far."

He stepped out, and I started to follow him, but had a second thought as the streetcar pulled away from the stop. He was already walking away as I started the car again. He turned back and opened his mouth to say something.

"You take him, Cap," I called through the open window. "I've got a hunch."

I glanced at him in the mirror as I drove off. His mouth was moving, but I couldn't catch what he was saying. I had a pretty good guess.

Chapter Seventeen

I was lucky the traffic was thin—I had to run two stop signs and a red light to catch up to the car. My hunch paid off when it stopped at Main. The first person out was a man in a tan raincoat and black-banded gray hat. He gave a quick look around, and his hand went up to his chest. I was sure he was adjusting something under his coat. I watched from a distance as the guy walked down Main. He moved with a quick step and looked back a couple of times, but didn't seem overly nervous. I let two other cars pass me by and fell in behind them. I drove past the guy and kept watch in the mirror. At the end of the block, I pulled into a small lot next to a drug store. I snapped on Monte's leash, and we got out of the car.

Our guy turned down a side street, and we followed at a discreet distance. It was a nice night, and a few people were out—a couple of them sitting on porches in front of little tract houses, and three young guys lounging on a car in front of another one, smoking and talking baseball.

Halfway up the block, the bird in the raincoat crossed the street and went up the steps into a little rooming house. I walked Monte past the place and stopped in the shade of a tree between the streetlamps. Through the half-glassed front door, I saw the guy climbing the stairs. Seconds later, a light came on in a second-floor window.

I saw a shadow behind the curtains before they parted. Then I caught a quick glimpse of the guy himself as he raised the window a couple of inches. He pulled the curtains closed again, and I watched his shadow as he took off his hat and coat and moved out of view.

I was about to hotfoot it back to the drugstore and call Decker to send out the troops when there was a flash behind the curtains, along with a gunshot. I unhooked Monte, and we hustled across the street and into the place.

Monte scrambled past me up the stairs and waited for me at the landing. I told him to stay, hit the door on the left, and went on through. I stood in a small, dingy room, cheaply furnished like places of that type always are. The man we'd followed was stretched out half on, half off a frayed rug near the middle of the floor. Blood was spreading across the front of his shirt, and he was trying without much luck to get up. Monte, obedient as ever, rushed in past me. He sniffed at the wounded man, then looked up at me with a nervous thump of his tail.

"Easy, pal." I wasn't sure which of them I was talking to. I knelt down next to the guy for a closer look. He'd been shot just right of center, and blood bubbled on his lips. He strained to focus his eyes on me and tried to speak. "Take it easy," I said again.

I went through the place as quickly as I could to make sure we were alone. There was a small bedroom, a bathroom, and a kitchenette off the tiny living room. A door off the kitchen was ajar, and led to a dim little landing and a flight of stairs down to the back yard. Whoever had shot the guy had used those stairs and was in the wind.

I found a phone in the kitchen and made a quick call to Decker, then wet a dish towel and went back to do what I could for the guy. His coat was draped over the back of the sofa, and an empty manila envelope lay on a side table. No cash in sight.

I held the towel as tight as I could against the wound in his chest. His breath wheezed, and he stared up at me. He gagged and spit out a mouthful of frothy blood.

"Shot me," he said weakly. "The b-bastard."

"I see that. Where's the girl?"

"Gone." He winced like the single word pained him.

"Gone where?"

"Took her—" he spit out more blood. His voice was fading, and I could see he wasn't going to last. He raised his head an inch, hacked, and his words came out in a wet, gurgling sound. "Took her to…" His voice dropped to a weak whisper, and when he spoke I wasn't sure I'd heard him right.

"Old Glenn's?" I asked him.

He gave his head a slight shake and tried to say something else, but only gave out with a faint whistling sound. His head dropped back, and he let out a long, final breath.

Y. Y. Y.

"What about the other two guys?" I asked Queenan. He and Dusty and I stood on the lawn in front of the rooming house while Decker and a couple of lab boys went through the rooms upstairs. Monte lounged beside us on the grass.

Queenan shook his head. "Just ringers, I guess. Couple of scratch house bums. A guy—" he jerked his chin toward the upstairs, "this same bird from the sound of it—picked 'em up in some crumb joint downtown, paid 'em a sawbuck each to ride the streetcar decked out in hats and coats he gave 'em. They didn't ask no questions. We'll hold 'em for now, ride 'em around the horn. But I don't think they know squat."

"Are we sure Beth was even here?"

"Pretty sure." He made a disgusted face. "Sanitary napkin in a wastebasket up there. It's a cinch it don't belong to your dead crook."

"What about Glenn's house?"

"Nada," he said. "I got a couple of men goin' through it, but no sign. It don't figure anyway—what would they take her there for? The guy's been cold meat for days. You're sure that's what he said—'old Glenn's'?"

"I can't be certain, but that's what it sounded like. No sign of the money?"

He shot his hands apart like a magician. "Gone. We'll print the envelope, but careful as these guys have been, I'm not getting' my hopes up."

"Anybody told Audrey Chase yet?"

"Yeah. You can guess she's pretty rattled. I borrowed a skirt copper from juvie to keep her company, and she had a doctor give Chase somethin' to calm her down. Meanwhile, we're still sittin' on her phone in case these mutts call again."

"Anything come of the phone trace?"

"Nothin' helpful. The call came in from a pay phone at Union Station. It ain't like those get used more than a thousand times a day. No point in our wastin' time with prints there—two dozen people probably handled the phone before we got to it."

"Damn." I shook my head. "Do you think these guys have got their money and this chump was just a loose end?"

"Who knows? It looks screwy to me. But I guess we'll just have to see what we see." Something in the way he said that perked up my ears.

"What *are* you thinking here, Cap?"

He stared at me for a long moment before he answered. "Has it crossed your mind," he said at last, "that the Chase girl herself might have dummied up this whole kidnap business?"

I started to respond, and he held up a hand. "Here's the thing. I guess it don't surprise you to hear that the coroner says Glenn really was dead drunk when he did his somersault down the stairs."

"Yeah…so?"

"So nobody had to toss him. That soused, a hot fart woulda blown him down the steps. It coulda been anybody."

"And you're thinking Beth…?"

"You told me she was plannin' on asking him for money. And she thought she was going to come into the cush when he died. Supposin' she found out there wasn't no cush—no pot of gold at the end of his rainbow. Maybe she puts him down and decides to tap her sister instead. Get what she thinks is comin' to her."

"That's quite a stretch, Cap. Are you saying you think she gunned this character, too?"

"I'm sayin' it could be, that's all. Now I know you got it bad for the sister, and she's been put through it, and you don't want to think she's bein' taken for a ride, but—"

"You're off your rocker, Queenan!" There had been plenty of times I'd wanted to belt him, but I'd never felt so close to doing it. He and Dusty must have both sensed it—he took a half step back, and Dusty laid a firm hand on my shoulder. Even Monte moved closer and pressed up against my legs.

Queenan showed me his palms. "Look, Ross, just think about it, that's all I'm sayin'. It's been a hell of a night. Go home, get some rest, and let's see where we are in the morning."

* * *

I considered driving up to check on Audrey, but as late as it was, I was sure she'd be asleep, especially if they'd had to sedate her. I settled for calling the house when I got home. I talked to the policewoman Queenan had sent over, and she said that Audrey was pretty frantic when Decker had told her what had happened, but that the doctor had examined her and was convinced that, physically at least, she was sound. She said Audrey had seemed better by the time she went to bed and that she was sleeping peacefully.

I asked her to reassure Audrey when she woke that Queenan and I were convinced that the kidnappers had gotten what they were after and would soon be in touch to arrange for Beth's return. There wasn't much truth, if any, in the statement, but I wasn't about to tell her what my gut was telling me. I was careful with what I said because I knew Queenan's coppers were listening in, and I wasn't in the mood for any more guff from him.

I'd forgotten to ask Queenan if anyone had given Jimmy Singer the news. I thought about calling the kid's house, but it was just as late in the poorer neighborhoods as it was in the rich ones. Morning would be soon enough—it wasn't as if any of what had happened would have changed.

I didn't get much sleep, and after a while I gave up trying. My mind was too busy for sleep. A small part of it was hoping for the best, and the rest was expecting the worst.

Chapter Eighteen

I showered but skipped the shave and breakfast. I wasn't hungry, and I didn't give a damn what face I showed the world today. I watched Monte eat his own breakfast with his normal gusto and felt a twinge of envy. What a simple life a dog like him had. Eat, sleep, crap. Few needs and fewer worries.

I was glad to find no Queenan waiting at my doorstep when we got to the office. It didn't mean good news, but it probably meant there was no bad news. Most likely, it meant there was no news. In any case, I was still nursing a beef with him and didn't feel like taking it up again that early in the day.

I did hear from Aggie Underwood. She'd gotten wind—only she and God knew how—that we'd come up snake eyes on the two ransom drops. She didn't seem to know, and I wasn't about to clue her in, that the thirty thousand was missing. She tried for ten minutes to wheedle some juicy information out of me, and when I wouldn't play, she told me what she thought of me and my entire family tree and hung up in a huff.

Once my ears had stopped ringing, I called Dusty at the bar. He sounded fresh and chipper and must have slept better than I did. It annoyed me a little, but I tried not to let it show.

"You're soundin' a might grouchy this morning," he said. So much for my efforts. "Still hankerin' to pull Queenan's ears off?"

"Ask me after I see him,"

"I don't think he meant nothin', Nate."

"Bullshit. You know him better than that."

"Maybe. Anyway, you don't sound like you got any news to report, so what's on your mind?"

"I need to talk to Walt."

Much as I wanted to give it the horse laugh, I'd been thinking over what Queenan had said about Beth. I still thought it was a lot of gas, but it did make me more curious to know just what Griffin Glenn's estate—whatever it might be—amounted to. I couldn't see how he could be involved in a kidnapping that had happened after he was dead, and I wasn't all that interested in who had killed him. But I kept thinking back to a Latin phrase I'd read in college—in my one criminology course. *Sequere pecuniam.* Follow the money. I couldn't shake the suspicion that Glenn's will might just hold some clue to both of those crimes.

Queenan was playing foxy with any information about the will. But I'd gotten a peek at his notebook when he'd opened it and saw the name *Carter Frazier* scribbled on a page. I'd checked the phone book and found an attorney named Carter Frazier who had an office on Temple. Specializing in wills and probates, the listing said. I knew talking to him would get me nothing—he'd drop the *confidentiality* line on me before I got the first question out. But as my old man liked to say, there's more than one way to skin a lawyer.

I dialed the number Dusty gave me, and the receptionist answered the phone by rattling off what I guessed was the full name of the firm. I caught *Ogden*, but she followed with more names than I could keep up with. If *VanNeer* was one of them, I lost it in the shuffle.

"Walter VanNeer, please," I said when she had paused to take in some air. Walt used his old man's original last name instead of Dusty's cowboyfied version, *Vanner*.

Walt answered with his own name, and I was thankful he'd skipped all the partners. Long distance wasn't cheap.

"How's Arizona?" I asked him. "Seen any Apaches yet?"

"Nate Ross—how the hell are you?" He had his dad's hearty way of talking and most of his Texas accent.

"Same as ever. Your old man says to tell you hello."

"I'm pretty sure he said *howdy*."

"Yeah, I'm paraphrasing."

"What do you need me to do?"

"I can't just call a pal to see how he's getting along?"

"You could, but you wouldn't. Let's have it."

I told him about Griffin Glenn, skipping most of the details. I gave him the phone number for Carter Frazier.

"I just thought maybe lawyer-to-lawyer he might loosen up a little."

"Well, it'd be better if I knew him personally, but I'll give it a try. I can't promise you anything."

"Whatever you can do." Since I knew that lawyers count their time in dollars, I didn't hold him up. He made me promise not to let his pop do anything too dangerous—Dusty was still mending after being shot in a robbery of sorts—and we said *adios*.

* * *

I still wasn't hungry, but went down to the diner and arranged with Benjy to keep an eye on Monte for a while. I needed to go see Jimmy Singer, and after their first meeting, Monte seemed to spook the kid. I drove to his house, but no dice there. No Jimmy, no Jimmy's mother.

Just to cover bases, I tried the seedy little hotel near Echo Park. There was a new clerk on duty—a young guy who wore a permanent sneer to go with his pompous manners. He stared at me down his nose and informed me that the young couple who had occupied room four had vacated some days ago, leaving no forwarding address.

"May I assist you further?" he asked in a tone that said it would definitely *not* be his pleasure.

"You could maybe ease up on the starch, Fauntleroy," I told him. "You're not clerking at the Biltmore, you know." His frosty gaze followed me out the door.

I didn't have anywhere else to look for Jimmy. It occurred to me that maybe he'd gone to see Queenan to find out how the drop had gone. I still wasn't feeling much like listening to Queenan and his theories and his needling, but Audrey was relying on us to bring Beth back to her. I thought about driving up to check on her first, but decided against it. Much as I wanted to see her, I didn't want to show up until I had good news. Or some news at least. So I took a deep breath, shoved all my irritation with Queenan to the back of my mind, and headed his way.

* * *

I walked in to find Queenan behind his desk, barking orders at somebody on the phone. Decker sat on a chair facing the desk, a file folder lying across his knees. He was leaning forward and looking like he wished Queenan would get off the phone.

Queenan tensed a little when he looked up and saw me coming in. If he thought I was there to plug him one, he made no effort to beat me to the draw. Decker and I swapped silent hellos, and I took the chair next to him.

"And I'm not jokin'!" With that final shot, Queenan dropped the receiver on the hook. His eyes flicked across me, he mumbled a curt "Mornin', Ross," and looked at Decker. "What have you got, Clyde?"

Decker held up the file. "Our dead hood's name is Binny Landis. You might remember him."

"Benny Landis?" Queenan screwed his face up in thought. It looked like it was painful to him.

"*Binny*," Decker repeated. He consulted the file. "Short for *Binford*. Binford Wellesley Landis."

"Good God all Friday!" Queenan said. "A handle like that, maybe whoever popped him done him a favor."

"Anyway," Decker went on, "we put the crimp on the guy a few years back. He had a slimeball racket, him and a partner. They'd get friendly with society girls, little jailbait daughters and college kids whose daddies had heavy pockets and images to keep up. They'd get the little dollies nicely drunk, talk 'em into posing for snapshots wearing nothing but loopy grins, then hold the old men up for whatever the market would bear."

"Okay, okay." Queenan snapped his fat fingers. "I kinda remember it now—the caper, not the names. We sent those babies up north, if I recall."

Decker nodded. "Folsom. Drew a dime, both of them."

"Lemme guess," Queenan said. "The sob sisters on the parole board bought their touching tales of regret and redemption." He struck a comic pose with his hand over his heart.

"Bingo, Cap. Binny's been out on parole since late '37." He looked over a couple of pages in the file. "Looks like he's been keeping the nose clean since then. On paper, anyway."

"Yeah, doin' the low crawl, you mean."

"You think maybe he was just another hired hand, like those two mopes we brought in?"

Queenan started to answer, but checked himself. He looked at me like he had just remembered I was sitting there. "What do you think, Ross?"

I tended to be suspicious whenever Queenan asked my opinion, especially in front of anyone else. He normally used it as an excuse to razz me. But I had a notion that this time he was actually holding out an olive branch. And I knew it was as close to an apology as I'd ever get from him.

I shook my head. "I don't see these guys trusting some street flunky to be their go-between. Not with thirty thousand cash on the line. Too likely that they'd never see him or their money. No, I'd say this Landis was a bona fide part of the crew."

Queenan nodded. "I'm of the same mind. Which leaves us with the question of *who*. Who smoked him and vamoosed with the cash? Partner looking to grab all the berries?"

"Why wouldn't the partner just make the pickup himself?" Decker put in. "That way, he'd already have the money safe in hand."

"And then he," Queenan gave me a deadpan stare, "or *she* could scrape old Binny off any time.

He just couldn't resist, I guess. I kept my trap shut and just shrugged in agreement.

"But for all we know," Decker added, "Binny was the one running the show, and it was a junior partner who grabbed the brass ring."

Queenan leaned back and cracked his knobby knuckles. "That could be, too, I guess." He watched me out of the corner of his eye to see if his crack had hit home.

When he saw I wasn't going to bite, he leaned forward again and put his hands flat on the desk. He looked down at them as he spoke. "Well, all this speculating ain't gonna move us forward. We don't know yet whether these shitbirds have their money or don't. And if they don't, we don't know what their next play will be. Until we do know something more, let's work on maybe figurin' out who all's in the sandbox." He looked at Decker. "Who was Landis's partner in his dirty pictures racket?"

Decker turned a few more pages. "A guy named Roy Stuckey. Twenty-four—I guess he'd be closer to thirty now. Also paroled in '37. Got a juvie record and a lot of general mopery stuff as an adult—B&E, shoplift, drunk and disorderly, a couple of gambling beefs. The extortion grift is his only felony rap." He looked up. "Not really the type you'd expect to boss a caper like this."

"But maybe, like you said, Binny was runnin' things and this guy's just the little brother."

Decker thumped the file. "Still, it sounds like Stuckey's stuff was all lightweight—nothing violent. Not so much as an assault charge. Doesn't sound like a guy who'd gun out his partner."

"Maybe, maybe not," Queenan said. "Thirty thousand in green is liable to give anybody's trigger finger the itch. Pull his whole jacket and the case file on his racket with Landis."

"Whatever you say, Cap." He flipped the file closed and stood up. "Meanwhile, I've got Valverde and Deacon up at the Chase place. Deke will let us know as soon as any new calls come in." Queenan made the *okay* sign, and Decker gave us both a nod and left.

Queenan fussed around with a sheaf of papers on his desk. He seemed to be waiting for me to say something. When I didn't, he spoke up without taking his eyes off the papers.

"You talk to Audrey Chase this morning?" he asked in what was supposed to sound like a casual voice.

"Not yet. Nothing to report that she hasn't already heard."

"I was thinkin' more along the lines of..." He looked up at me. "You know what? Never mind." He stacked the papers and laid them aside. "How about the Singer kid?"

"I tried. He hasn't been to school since this mess started. Nobody at the house. That bothers me a little."

"You don't think maybe he hung around last night? Put his nose in somehow, got himself jammed up?"

"I'm not sure what to think. He might have gone up to Audrey's, I guess."

"Nah. Decker just came from there. He would have mentioned it." He trimmed and lit a cigar, watched me through the smoke. "You haven't talked to her or the kid, what is it brings you in here so bright and early?"

"A couple of things. I wanted to find out if there was any word yet from the kidnappers."

"Like Decker says, not a peep. I don't know whether that's good news or bad."

"You'd think whether they have their money or not, they'd have been in touch by now."

"You'd think that. If it *was* them who scratched this Landis character, maybe they're just being cautious, sniffin' the air."

"Maybe."

"Well?" he said after a long pause, "What's the other thing?"

I took a deep breath. "I wanted to get things clear with you about Audrey Chase."

He leaned back and held up both hands. "Look, your business is your business. All I care about is that it don't fog up your head now that we're workin' together. It's lookin' like we're dealin' with some dangerous types here after all."

"Fair enough, Cap. But just for the record, and once and for all, she's a client. That's it."

He dropped his hands. "Okay, Ross. Case closed. Tell me what's on your docket until we hear from these mutts."

"I still need to run down Jimmy Singer, I guess, make sure he's okay. But if you're going to talk to this Roy Stuckey, I'd like to be in on that."

"We've gotta find him first. With any luck, he's back living in L.A. Parole should have his current info. I'll call you when I know. If I can't reach you, I'll call Vanner."

"Okay, and same if you get any calls from our body snatchers."

"You got it."

Chapter Nineteen

I drove back to the Singer house, but there was still nobody home. The next-door neighbor was out front with a watering can, dousing her flower beds. I got from her the name of the family that Muriel Singer worked for. I checked my street directory and found an address in Westwood.

The house wasn't half the size of Audrey Chase's place, but it still said heavy money. It was one of those Georgian affairs with a portico entrance and double front doors I could have gotten my car through sideways. The front lawn looked like it had been trimmed with nail clippers, one blade of grass at a time.

The framework around the doors was so ornate that if there was a doorbell in there, I couldn't spot it. I used the huge brass knocker and gave the heavy door four big raps. Muriel Singer opened the door with a polite, deferential look on her face. It vanished as soon as she recognized me.

"What do you want?" She looked me up and down with sullen eyes. "Come here to waste my time with more fairy tales?"

"I need to talk to you, Mrs. Singer. About Jimmy. It's important."

She hesitated, and I thought for a second she was going to shut the door in my face. But she shot a glance over her shoulder, then back at me. "You're lucky the folks are in the city right now. I can give you a few minutes—I'm still working."

She led me down a hallway to the back of the house and into the kitchen. We took chairs facing each other across the table.

"You're no cop," she said. "I saw your picture in the paper."

"If you read the story that went with it, you know why I couldn't tell you what it was all about."

"I guess. I still don't like being made a monkey of."

"Well, to be fair, you lied to me, too. Jimmy told me you knew that they'd headed off to get married."

Something changed in her look. The hostility faded, and curiosity seeped in. "You've talked to Jimmy?"

"He hasn't told you?"

She gave me a pitying look and spoke like she would to a five-year-old. "He's eighteen, and I'm his mother. So now he knows everything, and I don't know anything. He doesn't tell me much these days."

I told her the whole tale, from Jimmy and Beth's pretend kidnapping up through Jimmy's making the ransom drop and the pickup man's being put out of somebody's way.

She listened, open-mouthed. "My God. I didn't know any of this, I swear."

"But you knew he was eloping?"

"Only because I overheard him talking about it."

"Did you try and talk him out of it?"

"At first I did. I told him he should wait until he was older, until he had a job. Until he was sure, you know?"

"What do you mean 'at first'?"

She took a sudden interest in her fingernails. She gnawed her bottom lip and didn't say anything for several seconds. When she did, I had to strain to hear her.

"When he told me who the girl—who her sister—was…" She looked up at me with hot eyes and snapped, "You can think whatever you want about it, mister. If my boy had a chance to marry into a family like that…" The flash of anger faded, and she looked down again. "But I never would have thought it'd end up like this."

"It's not over yet."

She raised her eyes again. "You really think they'll let her go?"

"Once they get what they want, I think they will." It was only half a lie. "Anyway, we're hoping to find them first."

"Does Jimmy know?" she asked, "About the man being killed, and the ransom money gone?"

"I don't think so. That's why I'm trying to find him."

"You've tried the house?"

"I just came from there."

She shook her head. "He was home when I left for work this morning. Still sleeping—he came in pretty late last night."

"How late?"

"I'm not sure. After eleven, anyway. I was already in bed."

"Is that unusual?"

"Not really. He goes to clubs sometimes. I mean, he's only eighteen, but you know there are places..."

"Do you have any idea where he might be right now?"

She turned up her palms. "I wish I could tell you. After a while, you learn not to ask questions. It keeps the peace." She leaned in, concerned. "You don't think he's in danger?"

"I doubt it." Another half lie. "I just need to speak with him." I gave her a card. "If you see him before I do..."

"Okay." She tucked the card into a pocket and stood up. "Sorry, but I really have to get back to work. Will you call me if you find Jimmy? I'll be home around five."

I said I would, and she saw me to the door. She stood in the huge doorway watching as I drove away.

* * *

Back at the office, I called Audrey's, but she was out walking the grounds. Probably needed the fresh air. I talked to Valverde, one of the city's dicks on duty. He said she seemed to be feeling better, and that the phone line was still silent.

Benjy had taken Monte down to the diner where he was overfeeding him, I had no doubt. I was feeling pretty peckish by then myself, so I dropped in for some lunch and to relieve Benjy from his dog-sitting duty. He told me Monte was in the back room. Halfway through a hambone, if I knew Benjy.

"I've been reading all about the kidnap business," he said as he poured the coffee. He read all the city's newspapers front to back every single day and was always well informed and eager to talk with anyone about crime and politics. In L.A., of course, it was hard to separate the two.

"I guess it's all pretty hush-hush," he went on, "and you can't tell me much…" He gave me a hopeful look.

I just grinned in return, and he took the hint. "Just tell me one thing, though." He leaned in confidentially and dropped his voice. "Is that Audrey Chase as much of a dish in person as she is on the screen?"

"Pictures don't do her justice, pal."

"Holy smokes." He set the pot down and pulled out his order pad. "You have all the luck, Mr. Ross."

"Sure, that's me all over, kid. Why don't you hit me with the ham and rye?"

I'd finished the sandwich and was halfway through the potato salad when the phone rang, and Benjy came out of the kitchen, wiping his hands on his apron.

"Gus's Diner," he said into the mouthpiece. "Today's special is the…how's that? Sure, just a second." He held the receiver at arm's length. "For you, Mr. Ross."

I took a last bite and went to the phone. "Yeah?"

"I was hopin' you'd be there, Ross." Queenan's excited voice was like a trombone blast in my ear. "We just got a new phone call. Our babies didn't collect their money—or claim they didn't—and they're plenty steamed. The caller says since Chase made the drop in good faith, they'll give her, and the girl, one last chance. Mighty generous—like these assholes know the first thing about good faith. But maybe not that generous after all, since they expect her to pony up another thirty large.

"Shit. Sixty grand? You get anywhere on this Stuckey bird?"

"Not yet. Decker was workin' on it when this came in. How about your end—you find the Singer pup?"

"No, still in the breeze."

"Well, dance on over here, and I'll give you the rest of it."

"On my way." I hung up. Benjy gave me a curious look. "Hey, pal," I said.

"Would you mind…"

"Not a problem, boss. Go."

* * *

Queenan already had his hat on when I walked in. "Come on, Ross. I'll give you the scoop on the way. We can take my bus."

"Mine's faster."

"But mine don't have to stop at lights."

He filled me in as he steered the big black sedan up the twisting road. The same caller as before, but this time instead of talking to Audrey, he demanded to speak to "whatever copper's listening in." Deacon took over, and the caller at first accused the police of gunning down the pickup man. Deacon was able to convince him that the drop had gone off exactly as ordered and that whatever happened was not because of any play by the cops.

The caller insisted that there had been no monkey business on his end either, and that if it wasn't the police, he had no idea who'd killed his runner. He said that under the circumstances, he was willing to give Audrey Chase the benefit of the doubt, but that the lost money was her problem, not his.

"Now this guy's demandin' another load of cash," Queenan said. "And this time, he wants Audrey Chase to make the delivery in person."

I didn't like the sound of that. "I'm guessing he's not asking her to hide it in a men's room?"

"How I wish," he said. "Angel's Flight."

Chapter Twenty

ecker had arrived ahead of us and was standing out in front of the house when we pulled up, conversing with Spencer. The chauffeur gave us a polite nod as I got out of the car. He looked haggard and worried. There was no Mrs. Borne to meet us at the door as we filed in. Decker said that she and Vera Busic, the policewoman assigned, were tending to Audrey. She'd had to be sedated again after this latest phone call.

That meant I wouldn't be able to talk to her, but I wanted at least to look in on her. Decker directed me to the master bedroom, and I saw him and Queenan exchange knowing looks as I went up the stairs. Busic was coming out of the room as I walked down the hallway. She wasn't who I'd pictured from the phone call. She was tall and lean, fortyish, with light hair just starting to go gray. The tight bun hairdo and wire rim glasses made her look more like a librarian than a cop. But the crisp uniform, the confident voice, and the steely eyes behind the specs told a different story.

Since we'd only talked on the phone, I introduced myself, and she offered a sturdy handshake. She told me that Audrey was sleeping. We walked to the doorway, and I could see Audrey lying in a huge canopy bed against the far wall. Mrs. Borne sat beside her, her back to us. Audrey's breathing was deep and even—a drugged sleep—and she looked pale and had dark patches under her eyes.

Busic looked at Audrey and shook her head. "She took this last call extra hard," she said in a low voice. "I don't know if all this is just wearing her down, or if it's because they expect her to bring the money herself." She turned her steady gaze on me. "I honestly don't know if she's going to be up to that."

I shrugged. "The hell of it is, we don't have much choice. This thing has gone sideways on us twice already. I'm hoping the third time's the charm, because I doubt they are going to give us another chance."

Busic shook her head, looked at Audrey again. "Poor woman. It's not like the movies."

"No, it's sure as hell not."

"I'll see if we can get her to eat something when she wakes up. Maybe if she gets her strength up a little…" She turned back to me. "I'll give her my best pep talk."

"Thanks," I said.

I headed back downstairs and found Queenan and his boys sitting around the living room.

"How's the client?" Queenan asked.

"Sleeping. Busic's not sure she's going to hold up for this game." I took an empty chair.

"I hope she's wrong," he said. "If this deal goes sour again…" He let the possibilities hang in the air.

"I told her as much. She'll do what she can."

"Good." He waved a hand. "Meantime, we've been talkin' things over, tryin' to get a bead on what and who we might be dealin' with. Deke here thinks this was all just a two-man team."

Deacon spoke up. "I'm convinced that from the get-go it's just been this dead turd Landis and Stuckey or whoever he's tied in with. According to Miss Chase, the same guy has made all three calls. Obviously, it wasn't Landis."

Valverde snickered. "That'd be a cute trick."

Deacon looked a little annoyed by the interruption. "Anyway, in the first two calls, the guy on the phone said 'we'. This last one, he said, 'I'. 'I don't want no tricks'—his exact words."

"Now that Ross is here," Queenan said to him, "Run down again how this drop's supposed to go."

Deacon turned in his seat to face me. "Like you already know, our guy wants Miss Chase to carry the money. It's insurance, he says. Anything goes screwy, he sees us anywhere near, he says she'll catch a bullet before we can get to him. And we'll never see the girl again."

"Shit," I said. "No wonder the doc had to dose her."

"Yeah," Deacon went on. "Can't say I envy her. Anyway, she's to be there by eight, on the train, alone."

Angel's Flight wasn't a train in the normal sense. It was what they called a funicular railway—it ran up and down the steep slope of Bunker Hill between 3rd and Hill streets. There were two small cars, each with room for two dozen people, maybe three dozen if they sat elbow to elbow. While one car crawled up the twin track, the other would be coming down, and they'd cross in the middle. Then they'd reverse for the return trip.

"And does she leave the money, like before?" I asked him.

He shook his head. "He says someone—our boy himself, I'm guessing—will board the car at some point. She's to keep riding the car back and forth until he shows, and for fifteen minutes after he leaves. He says there'll be a gun on her the whole time, and if anything goes wrong or she gets off the train early…" He fired a finger gun to make the point. "He says he'll call here when she gets home to tell us when and where to pick up her sister."

My stomach felt like I'd swallowed lead weights. I looked over at Queenan. "Just how are we planning on covering this thing?" Maybe I sounded more worried than I intended. All heads swiveled my way.

Queenan looked at me for a long time. "Let's you and me discuss that on the drive back." He looked at the others. "With Landis out of the game like Deacon said, let's figure maybe we're playin' with a lone operator now."

"Roy Stuckey?" Valverde put in.

"Maybe. I'd say even probably." He looked at Decker. "Why don't you stay on that angle? Round up whatever we have on him and get with parole, see if he's still around."

"Got it, Cap."

Queenan turned to Deacon, "How about the trace on this latest phone call?"

"Just got off the horn with the exchange. It came from a pay phone at the Greyhound station at 6th and Los Angeles." He shook his head with frustration. "First Union Station, now the bus depot. I think the son of a bitch is playing games with us. Wants us to think they're—or he's—moving the girl around."

"He put her on the phone this time?"

"Nope."

Queenan scratched his jaw. "Not sure I like the sound of that. Then again, if he's workin' solo now, he's probably not keen to take her out and about. Too much chance of her takin' it on the run, and with all this press, too much risk of being spotted.

The three detectives all nodded their agreement. Decker stood up. "I'm going to head back to the clubhouse, Cap. Get back to work on our friend Stuckey."

"Yeah, okay." He turned to Deacon and Valverde. "One of you boys stay here in case there's any more phone traffic, and one of you go with Decker. Pull the latest mugshot we got of Stuckey and go show it around at the bus station. Maybe we get lucky, find someone who IDs him."

"I'll do it, Cap," Valverde said. "Deke's been managing the phone."

"Okay, let's breeze then." Queenan got up and put his hat on. "Let's meet up back here at six."

* * *

"Why the private talk, Cap?" I asked Queenan as we glided back down the hill. "What don't you want your boys to know?"

"It ain't that." He didn't even glance at me. I read something more than careful driving into it. "I think maybe you need to sit this next part out, Ross."

It took me a few seconds to decide whether I'd heard him right. "Just what the hell does that mean?"

"Look." He pulled in a long breath through his nose. "I know I said your business is yours, and I meant it. But the way this thing's gotta go... You're a little hot and bothered, and this is gonna take clear heads and steady nerves. And no cowboyin'.

"And you don't think I can manage that?"

"I don't think your head's where it needs to be."

I started to answer that, but he cut me off. "No shame in it. I was in your shoes, I'd be in the same shape."

"You weren't worried about this before."

"The other two times was different. Your—*she's* on the spot this time around, and that changes everything. I don't like to pull the badge on you here, but this is a police operation. I can't afford to have this woman or one of my guys hurt or killed, and me have to answer for it. And have to live with it." He shot me a quick look. "And you gotta face facts, Ross. There's a chance this can go bad—I mean, real bad—and if it does, you don't wanna be there to see it."

What I *was* seeing just then was red, but I knew arguing with Queenan was a waste of time. I might as well argue with a lamppost. I kept my trap shut and stewed all the way back to my office.

As he stopped in the gravel lot, Queenan turned toward me. He put as much sympathy into his voice as he was capable of. "I know you got to do somethin' on this thing, or you'll go bughouse. Just keep workin' on findin' the Singer kid. We still need to know that he's all right, and he needs to know what's goin' on."

I got out of the car. Before I shut the door, I leaned in and met him eyeball to eyeball. "You'll let me know how it goes." It wasn't a question.

"First call I'll make."

I nodded, closed the door, and slapped the roof as he drove away.

I started into the building when I heard my name called. I turned and saw Benjy waving an arm and coming my way from the diner, hustling as fast as his long apron would allow.

"You okay, Mr. Ross?" he asked when he reached me. I guess he'd read my face—Benjy's a shrewd observer of human behavior.

"I'm fine, pal. What's the rush?"

He looked doubtful, but went ahead. "I had to take Monte up to your office. Uncle Gus was coming by, so…"

Gus Karavolos, the cranky old Greek who owned the diner, was opposed to letting dogs inside his fine eating establishment. Personally, I thought they gave the joint a much-needed touch of class.

"That's all right," I told Benjy. "He mostly just sleeps when he's up there."

"Well, anyway, while I was up there, you had a couple phone calls." He pulled a slip of paper from his pocket. "One from Miss Underwood and another from a lady named…" He squinted at the note. "Muriel Singer."

Chapter Twenty-One

I didn't feel like playing twenty questions with Aggie, and I wasn't about to hand her the latest developments. Not until we saw how they played out, anyway.

I gave Monte a scratch or two and refilled his water bowl, then dialed Muriel Singer's number. She answered on the second ring, and she sounded put out.

"I've been trying to call you," she said. "I rang your office four times."

I wasn't in any mood to be crabbed at, but I managed to keep my tone more or less civil. "Sorry, been out of the office most of the day."

"Well, you missed Jimmy."

"Jimmy came home?"

"An hour and a half ago. But he left again."

At least it sounded like the kid was still in one piece. "Did he say where he was going?"

That got me a harsh laugh. "I told you, he doesn't tell me anything. He just said he'd be back later."

"Did you tell him I was looking for him?"

"I did. He doesn't seem to like you much."

"No, we're great pals. It's my dog he doesn't like."

"Huh?"

"Never mind. Did he say anything about last night? Did he know anything about it?'

"Yes. It was in the paper. He said he read the whole thing."

"Is that all he said?"

There was a long pause. "*Nooo.*" She gave it two or three syllables. "No, that wasn't all."

"Okay, what else?" My patience was about spent.

"I mean, no offense, but…" Her voice was hesitant. "But he said, 'Those Keystone coppers are going to make a mess of the whole thing."

"Did he, now?" I couldn't help but laugh. I already hadn't been very much fond of young Jimmy. Cocky little bastard. "Well, you can tell him from me that the L.A. police and Nate Ross are on top of this thing, and it'll be over soon. Then he and his sweetheart can start living like a pair of adults and wishing to God they'd stayed in school where they belong."

The line was quiet. She didn't seem to know how to take my little rant or what to say. I felt like a sap for losing my temper, so I put on a gentler tone. "Look, Mrs. Singer, I'd still like to talk to Jimmy myself. Please call me when he comes home again, okay? Day or night."

"I'll try," she said.

After we hung up, I fired up a cigar and just sat and thought. I thought about calling Queenan to tell him I'd at least had word of Jimmy Singer, but the talk with him still rankled me. I was trying to work out what I wanted to do when I remembered that I needed to check back with Walt.

I rang his office, not sure if I'd find anyone in at that time of day. But I guess the law never sleeps. The same receptionist answered, and I had to listen to her rattle off the same cast of characters before I asked to speak to Walt.

"Hey, Nate," he said when we'd been connected. "Sorry I haven't gotten back to you. I've been run ragged tying up loose ends here before I head back to the land of eternal sunshine."

"Isn't Arizona a land of eternal sunshine?"

"Yeah, but we also have Gila monsters."

"Plenty of reptiles out here. They mostly make movies or practice law."

He laughed. "I ought to fit right in, then. Anyway," he went on, switching gears in his usual lawyerly wasting-no-time way, "I had a talk with Carter Frazier. Not a bad egg for an L.A. attorney—in fact, I might have just found my first job prospect, thank you very much. Seems like Griffin Glenn was even worse off than you thought. When you stack what little money he had against what he owed, he was nearly ten thousand dollars in the hole. And I'm only talking about legitimate debt, not gambling markers, and Frazier thinks there were plenty of those as well."

"What about a will?"

"Oh, yeah, he had one. God knows why. Sole heir named in it was Elizabeth Ruth Chase. Had her down as his 'goddaughter'. This help your case any?"

"It doesn't hurt it, anyway. Thanks, Walt."

I hung up and thought it over. Rumors and speculation about the sorry state of Glenn's finances had been right. If anything, they'd underestimated how bad off the guy was. I filed that away in my head for the time being and dialed Audrey's phone number. I wanted at least to talk to her before the ball opened, maybe reassure her a little. Let her know I was still on the job.

Mrs. Borne answered and handed the phone off to Vera Busic. She told me Audrey was awake and seemed to be doing better. She was downstairs, Busic said, talking with the detectives to get the plan for the drop down pat.

"I can get her if you want," she said. "I think they're just about through anyway."

"I'd appreciate it. And can you get Deacon or whoever's listening in to lay off for a few minutes?"

She chuckled. "I'll take care of it." She raised her voice a notch. "You hear that, Deke?" I heard a couple of clicks on the line, and Busic said, "Hold on just a minute, Nate."

I waited, thinking over exactly what I should say, what kind of reassurance I could even offer her.

"Hello, Nate." She sounded a little breathless. I wondered if it was from fear and anticipation, or maybe she'd just rushed up the stairs to take my call. I liked thinking it was that.

"How are you feeling, Audrey?"

She made a breathy sound that could have been a laugh or a sob. "I'm all right, considering. I'm ready to go through with this if it will end this horrible nightmare, if it brings Beth back home safe. But I don't mind telling you that I'm terrified."

"It's going to be okay," I told her. Even as the words left my mouth, I could hear how weak, how wishy-washy they sounded, and I gave myself a mental kick in the ass. I tried to find the words, hoping to salvage any chance of giving her something to help her through what promised to be a very tough night.

I started again. "Look, kid," I took a deep breath to buy me a little time. "You're in a cutthroat business, but you've managed to make it to the top. The very top. You weathered all that crap with Griffin Glenn and stood up to everything he and the newspapers threw at you when most people would have folded up their tents and done a fade out. That tells me, and it ought to tell you, that you're a whole lot tougher than you realize."

"But the stakes are higher here. This is literally life and death." Her laugh came without humor. "God, that sounds like a line from a bad movie script."

"The stakes are high, but the payoff is going to be worth it. And Queenan's got plenty of people looking out for you."

"It's not me I'm worried about, it's Beth."

"I know. But you'll have your girl back with you soon. For now, maybe that's how you get through tonight. Keep telling yourself it's just a part in a bad movie. It's not real—it's nothing but another acting job. Can you do that?"

"I'll try. And as long as I know you're there watching over me, I won't be nearly as afraid."

I'd been hoping that wouldn't come up. I didn't want to lie to her, but how could I tell her that Queenan was dealing me out?

"I'm sorry, Nate," she said, as I was trying to decide which wrong choice to make. "I have to go. Vera's telling me they need me back downstairs."

Saved by the bell. "Okay, kid. Listen to the cops, do just what they tell you, and we'll get out of this thing all right. And remember, it's only a movie."

"Thank you, Nate."

After a moment, Busic came back on the line. "The boys needed to hash out some last-minute details with her."

"How is she really? She gonna get through this all right?"

She didn't even hesitate. "I think she's going to be just fine."

"Are you going to be there to make sure?"

She laughed. "You're joking, right? They give me a badge and gun, but not much chance to use either one. No, I'm sitting this part out." She let out an angry breath. "You've no idea how that feels."

"You'd be surprised."

I started to hang up, but heard, "Oh, hey."

"Yeah?"

"Captain Queenan mentioned that you were trying to find the Singer boy. He came here maybe half an hour ago."

Damn slippery kid. "Is he still there?"

"No, came and went. Audrey didn't want to see him, but he talked to Valverde. Val brought him up to date."

"Okay, well, that's all I was looking to do, anyway. Thanks."

I sat for a while and thought about whether what I wanted to do was what I *should* do, and when I'd made up my mind, I went downstairs.

"Son of a bitch," I said to myself as I stared across the small gravel parking lot. I'd completely forgotten that I'd left my car at the police station. Had it just slipped Queenan's mind, too, or had he thought leaving me without my boat would help guarantee I'd stay out of his way? I had a pretty good idea which.

"Guess I'm going to see Queenan after all," I muttered to myself as I started hoofing down Hillhurst.

* * *

I had to walk three blocks to a streetcar stop and another two when I got off. My car was parked where I'd left it, and I was just going to get in and go, but thought as long as I was here I might as well take one more pass at Queenan and see if I could get an invite to the party.

It was late in the day, and there was nobody much left in the Detective Bureau. There was no one in Homicide but a mousy little clerk I'd never seen before. The lights were out in Queenan's office. The clerk gave me a meaningless smile, and I was about to leave when she stepped past me and went through Queenan's door. As she paused to turn on the light, I clocked the tab on the folder she was carrying. It read, "Stuckey, R."

I followed her in and turned on the Nate Ross smile. "Say, is that the Roy Stuckey file?" She turned and gave me an uncertain look. Lucky for me, I still had the juice badge in my pocket. I fished it out and gave it the flash. "DeMasse," I said. "Missing Persons. Captain Queenan asked me to stop by and take a look at that. Guess I just missed him."

She bought the gaff and handed me the folder. "Will you ask him to be sure he gets that back to Records?" She looked at the disorderly pile on his desk. "He's kind of bad about that sort of thing."

"I'll make sure he does," I told her with a wink. She went out and closed the door, and I listened to her heels clicking down the hallway.

I sat in Queenan's sprung swivel chair and opened the file. Clipped to the inside of the folder was a parole officer's business card. Penciled across the bottom, I read Stuckey's name and an address. Below that, it said, "No longer there. Current residence unknown". I wasn't surprised. I knew the place, a notorious flop for cons out on good time or lamsters looking to keep out of circulation. Nobody stayed in a place like that for long.

The file had Stuckey's mugshot from the extortion arrest a few years back. I thought I saw something familiar in the face, but couldn't peg it. You see a lot of mugs—and mugshots—in my trade. There was a spare copy I figured nobody would miss, so I pocketed it.

I read through the reports and looked at samples of the snapshots Stuckey and Landis had taken and turned into cash. Decker hadn't painted a nasty enough picture of their racket—they were definitely a couple of grade-A lowlifes. As Decker had suggested, I didn't see anything in the file to make me think Stuckey was a life-taker. But as Queenan had pointed out, with so much money on the line…

Almost the last thing, and the most interesting thing, I found in the file was a group of photos of the demand notes the two creeps had sent to wealthy fathers. Looking them over, I was almost sure I'd seen that handwriting before. When I went into my pocket again, I had no doubt.

Chapter Twenty-Two

The hill that Angel's Flight drags its way up is a steep incline rising beside and above the 3rd Street tunnel. The narrow twin track stretches for about three hundred feet and at its uphill end empties passengers out on to Olive Street. To walk the stairs up that hill took a strong heart and a sturdy pair of legs, which I guess was the whole reason for the little railway.

Along with leaving Monte with Benjy once more, I'd swapped my car for his. The kid's goodwill had no end. I knew Queenan would have his boys on the lookout for my bucket, even though one blue Ford looked about like another. But they weren't likely to make me driving Benjy's rusted old brown DeSoto. Normally, I wouldn't have ventured out in public in such an ugly car, but this was no time to indulge my vanity.

I parked Benjy's car on Olive at the top of the hill, half a block south of the entrance to Angel's Flight, then hopped out and took it on foot. I'd dressed in a ratty windbreaker jacket and old tweed cap and looked, or hoped I did, nothing like a cop. Much as I didn't want Queenan or his boys to spot me, I was more worried about spooking our kidnap artist into retreating. Or worse, into doing something we'd all regret.

I was familiar with the geography there and knew that several buildings of six or eight stories flanked the railway along its south side. Much the same on the north, but 3rd Street divided those buildings from Angel's Flight. If our boy wasn't conning us and he did have a shooter covering the railway cars, that's where he'd be. The angle from the south side buildings would be too steep for a clear shot. The cops would have figured that, too, which meant that they—most of them anyway—would be watching from the south side.

They'd also have to cover both entrances. The downhill one was pretty easy—there was a drugstore on the ground floor of the Ferguson Building, just across the narrow alleyway from the railway entrance. At the top end stood a tall observation tower with a platform on top. From up there, anyone would have a more-or-less bird's-eye view of the whole layout, but there was no quick way down unless he was willing to do a hundred-foot freefall. Plus, he'd be too easy to spot and a sitting duck. Too impractical and too risky.

The Elks lodge building, nearest the Olive Street entrance, had plenty of facing windows. It seemed the likely choice. A cop watching from in there wouldn't go any higher than the second floor. That meant I would have to watch my step and hope whoever was in there didn't know me on sight. Although at this point, if they did spot me there wasn't a hell of a lot they could do about it.

I'd stopped and bought a pint of cheap rye on the way over and left it in the brown paper bag. I opened it and started up the block, trying to put just enough stagger into my step. Ten feet past the ornate orange archway entrance to the train was a bus stop. Nobody was around. I stretched out on the bench, bottle clutched at my side.

Behind the bench and beyond the sidewalk, sparse hedges ran along a wire fence that enclosed a sort of parkway above the tunnel between the railway and the flight of stairs on the Hill Street side. By looking through the space between the bench's seat and back, I could look through a gap in the hedges and see both of Angel Flight's cars and the whole length of the track. I also had a decent view of the buildings facing 3rd Street on both sides.

I sneaked a look at my watch. 7:21. The caller had told Deacon to have Audrey on board with the money by eight, but there was no knowing exactly when he'd show up.

Fifteen minutes later, I'd watched the two tangerine-colored cars do their do-si-do a couple of times. It was well past business hours, and there weren't all that many people riding. I was glad of that—our guy surely wouldn't approach Audrey unless and until she was alone in the car, and there was no way of controlling that.

I knew Queenan would also have coppers on foot at both ends watching all comings and goings and taking careful note of anybody who looked wrong. After eight, they'd have to shadow anyone leaving who'd been in Audrey's car because there would be no way to know the pickup had been made until she left the car fifteen minutes later.

It was looking like I'd managed to avoid being spotted and wouldn't have to deal with one of the detectives trying to run me off. I was keeping close watch on the bottom of the hill, since I knew the plan was for Spencer to drop Audrey off at the curb right at the Hill Street entrance. The big blue Packard would be a cinch to spot.

Thus far, nobody had bothered me, and it looked like I'd be able to keep the bus stop to myself. Then I heard a sort of low, droning noise coming down the sidewalk. As it got closer and louder, I could tell it was singing, or was supposed to be. I raised my head for a nip at my pint and to give me an excuse to look and see who was coming.

A big, barrel-chested guy was weaving my way. He wore filthy, mismatched, and ill-fitting clothes and a tattered, greasy hat pulled low on his forehead. His hands and his face—what I could see of it—were covered with grime. He was half humming, half singing to himself in a low, slobbery voice. Guys like him boiled up out of nowhere at this time of night in downtown. Just my rotten luck, I had to have one come along now. For a second, I thought he would pass me by, but as he started past the bench he did a double take, took a stumbling backward step, and plopped his big rump down right on my left foot.

"Hey, pal, this seat's taken," I said through my teeth. I gave him a nudge with my other foot. "Go on, breeze."

He was a big boy. I figured in his condition, I could take him if it came to it, but not without drawing attention.

"Whatsa matter, bub?" he said without looking my way. His voice was thick and slurry. "There's plenty enough room for two."

Something in his voice reminded me of something, but I had no time to puzzle it out. I fished a five-dollar bill out of my pocket. "Look, buddy." I held out the bill. "Here's a fin to beat it and leave me my bench."

He lowered his chin to his chest and swung his big melon head around to look at me. "Bribin' a copper's a crime, Ross. You oughta know that."

"Queenan."

He pushed the hat back enough that I could see the evil glint in his eyes. "You just couldn't listen, could you?"

"How the hell—"

He chuckled. "For cryin' out loud, you think I don't know your moves by now?"

"You knew I'd be here?"

He nodded. "I would be if it'd been me."

Grabbing the bottle from my hand, he took a healthy swig and wiped his mouth on a grubby sleeve. He moved off my foot and slouched down at the end of the bench. With his legs sticking straight out, he threw an arm over the bench back and lay his head on the arm in an attitude of drunken slumber. With two such disreputable characters hogging the bench, I didn't think we'd have to worry about anybody coming too near the bus stop.

"We got this place sewed up but good," he said out of the corner of his mouth. "Covered six ways to Sunday." He ran down for me point-by-point where he had people positioned. About where I'd thought. "If we can spot this chump, we're in good shape to tail him wherever he heads from here."

"*If* we can spot him."

"They've all got pictures of Stuckey," he said, "in case it's him who shows. And don't worry, we got a signal all worked out with Chase. She's gonna be carryin' this little fur piece—fox stole or whatever. As soon as the money's handed off, she throws the thing around her shoulders, and that tells us that whoever gets off her car is our meat. Deacon's in the drugstore down the hill and Valverde's in one of the offices over here." He motioned with his head toward the big lodge building opposite the railway gate. "They get a phone call from one of the boys watchin' from the Ferguson or the other buildings, and they pick up the tail when the guy walks out."

That gave me a little more confidence. If all went according to Hoyle, we might actually have a chance of pinching this guy. And more importantly, get Beth Chase back unharmed.

Queenan's low rumble interrupted my thoughts. "Okay, looks like the show's about to start." I looked down the hill and could see the Packard limousine approaching on Hill Street. Halfway across 3rd it stopped to let a couple of pedestrians cross, then Spencer guided it to the curb in front of the Angel's Flight entrance. The entrance being right at the intersection, and the car being extra long, he had to pull ahead and stop in front of the drugstore, and the corner of the building mostly blocked out the view.

I tensed up a little at that, but Queenan muttered, "Don't worry. Deke will have 'em in sight. Anyway, there she is."

Audrey stepped around the corner of the building and came through the gaudy archway. She was dressed down, probably to avoid any undue attention from autograph hounds. She wore a simple maroon blazer and matching skirt, and a conservative black hat. She carried a small black handbag and a reddish fur stole draped over one arm. It had to be concealing the packet of cash.

She looked cool and unhurried as she waited for the cars to finish their current run. Maybe she had taken my advice to heart and was treating this whole adventure like a film role.

Riders on the contraption paid their fare to the operator at the top. I couldn't see him from my vantage point, but if it was the same bird as the last time I'd ridden, he was a grouchy old jasper who paid little attention to who got on or off, except to be sure he collected their coin or tickets. Whoever it was, he wouldn't be likely to be suspicious of a lone woman riding back and forth multiple times. Angel's Flight was a must-ride for tourists, and the city had more eccentrics than it had streetlights.

The current trip ended, and a straggle of people disembarked at each end. Audrey boarded along with three other people—a short, stocky guy in a derby hat, and a woman carrying a shopping bag and dragging a little boy by the hand. At our end, an elderly couple and three college kids got on board. The engine started whirring, and the two cars began clanking their way along the track toward each other.

"They got names, you know," Queenan said. "The two cars, I mean."

I shot him a look. It wasn't normally like him to make idle chit-chat, but he seemed to be making a habit of it lately. "I know," I answered. "Sinai and Olivet."

"Funny kind of names."

"From the Bible, if I recall my Sunday School lessons. A couple of pretty important mountains."

He shot me a look back. "I don't know whether I'm more surprised that you know that, or that you went to Sunday School." He looked back down the track again. "Well, I'd say we're sittin' on top of a pretty important hill right now." He watched the cars as they crossed in the middle. "I wonder which one's which?"

"No idea."

That seemed to exhaust the small talk for both of us. We watched in silence as the cars finished their run and a fresh handful of passengers paid their nickel fare and boarded. Queenan said that Audrey was going to pay for enough trips in advance that she'd have no need to get off the car again.

"Personally," he said, "I think the gag about the gun covering her is all bullshit. A bluff. But no point in takin' chances."

Nearly an hour went by, and nothing went on at all but the monotonous back and forth of the cars. The later it got, the fewer people who showed up to ride. My shoulder ached from the hard bench, and my legs were cramping from making room for Queenan's bulk. At a quarter past midnight, the ride would stop, and the operator would close up for the night. We could have a long wait. I started to wonder if we were going to come up empty a third time and what it would mean for Beth if we did.

The cars reached home again, and all the passengers but one left the cars. I caught a glimpse of Audrey's face as her car squealed to a stop at the top, and she still didn't show any sign that she was nervous. I guess I'd underestimated her acting talent.

Queenan made a low hissing noise, and when I looked his way, he jerked his chin toward our entrance. A guy was walking through the archway, looking furtively around him as he passed through. Young, not much more than a kid. Skinny, with a pale, scowling face. He had the look of a feral cat and the twitchy, restless eyes of a junkie. The eyes settled briefly on us, then moved on.

"That ain't Stuckey," Queenan murmured. "But he's on the prowl for sure."

This guy boarded the car behind two middle-aged Mexican ladies and took a seat directly across from them. They looked uneasy, and they both hugged their purses a little tighter. As the cars got underway, Audrey glanced at him without evident interest but shot a quick side-to-side glance up and down the track.

"Could be our boy," Queenan said. "Or could be he's gonna do a snatch-and-run as soon as that thing reaches bottom. *That's* all we need right now."

We watched and waited while the car made its slow descent. "Look alive down there, Deke," Queenan said through his teeth.

We both exhaled with relief when the cars stopped, and the hophead got out and went one way, while the two women went the other. I imagined that Audrey felt even more relieved.

On our end, a family of four passed through the gate—mother and father in their thirties, a high-school-aged boy, and a girl of about ten. At the bottom, only one person boarded, a man in horn-rimmed glasses and a natty brown suit and hat, smoking a pipe and carrying a briefcase.

Queenan looked at his watch, then looked side-long at me. "I don't like to think how this might go if we end up with an empty sack again."

We had a head-on view of Audrey's car as it rumbled back up the track. She and the briefcase guy appeared to be engaged in polite conversation. He was sitting back, relaxed. When they were close to the midpoint, he tapped his pipe out on the windowsill and pocketed it, then leaned forward like he was about to make an interesting point. He smiled under his dark mustache and said something, and Audrey nodded. Her hand slid out from under the fur in her lap, she handed him a bulky brown package, and he put it into his briefcase. As though she'd felt a sudden chill, Audrey draped the fur stole around her shoulders.

Queenan's eyes shot sideways to me and back, making sure I'd seen what he'd seen. "Hot damn," he said. "We got this baby now."

He'd no sooner spoken than the train passed the top of the tunnel where the parkway began. Our guy got up and stepped to the bottom end of the car and out through the doorway onto the little platform. He sidearmed the briefcase out over the parkway and down into the grass and brush nearly twenty feet below, then followed it with a feet-first leap.

He hit the ground below like a paratrooper, feet and knees together and a quick twist to the side. He rolled once, came up on his feet, snatched up the briefcase, and made for the low fence and stairway on the north side.

"Son of a bitch!" Queenan was on his feet and headed for the stairway. I followed at his heels, surprised at how quickly a guy his size—who had to be pushing fifty—could move. Looking downhill as I ran, I saw our guy clamber over the fence, dash across the stairway, and go through a door into one of the buildings.

Down on Hill, I saw three guys I was sure were Queenan's dodging through traffic as they ran across the street, and two more sprinting up the staircase toward us.

We met up at the doorway our circus-jumper had run through. The two coppers went in, then Queenan, then me. We were in the hallway of a hotel. We passed by a writing room, a smoking room, a barbershop, and a small store for necessities, plus a couple of stairways leading to rooms upstairs. At the end of the hallway, we reached a lobby with a double glass door leading out to 2nd street.

Queenan looked up toward the upper floors and huffed out an angry breath. "Motherless rat could be anywhere." Decker, Deacon, and three other coppers I didn't know had joined us by then. The desk clerk glared at us when we all spilled into the lobby. Queenan gave brisk orders to the cops to divide up—three to take the upper floors and two to check the ground floor rooms.

I stayed in the lobby with Queenan. The clerk looked with distaste at our appearance. His look changed to alarm when Queenan stomped straight over to the desk, pointing his thick forefinger like a gun. "Hey, you!"

The guy took a step back. I was sure he thought he was about to be beaten and robbed. Queenan made an impatient noise and pulled out his shield. "Easy now, sunshine. We're police. You see a guy come through here and go out that way?" He pointed to the glass doors. "Not more than two, three minutes ago?"

The clerk still looked uncertain but managed a weak nod.

"Medium height and build? Dark mustache, brown suit and hat, luggin' a briefcase?"

The clerk worked his mouth a little, finally found his voice. "No, sir. He had a mustache, yes, but no coat or hat. And no briefcase."

"Guest of the hotel?"

"I couldn't say, sir. I only just came on duty. He's not a person I've seen before, if that helps."

Queenan turned with a growl and smacked a fist into his palm. Just then, Deacon and one of the other cops came out of the hallway. Deacon was carrying a briefcase with his handkerchief wrapped around the handle. Mud and a few blades of grass stuck to one corner.

"Found it in the men's room next to the barber shop," he said. "Shoved behind the toilet. Got a brown suit coat and hat crumpled up inside."

"And lemme guess," Queenan fumed. "No envelope full of dough?"

Deacon shook his head. Queenan spun on the desk clerk, causing him to turn pale all over again. "This guy you saw come through here. Which way did he head?"

Chapter Twenty-Three

We spent the better part of an hour looking, with no luck at all. Queenan's boys went through the entire hotel, top to bottom. No dice. It seemed a cinch that the guy the desk clerk had seen going out was out man, but nobody else seemed to have seen him. The clerk told Queenan the guy had walked west on 2nd, so we started there. But after talking to every business owner, cab driver, every worker and customer in every restaurant and bar on the block, we came up with exactly nothing.

I stopped at a phone booth and made a quick call to Audrey's number. She'd already turned in—I couldn't blame her—but I wanted to see how she was holding up. Busic said that she'd been in fairly good spirits when Spencer brought her home, and seemed to feel that the worst was over now. I wished I could be as optimistic.

Valverde had followed Spencer home, and he'd already briefed Busic on how things went at Angel's Flight. She sounded just as angry and frustrated as the rest of us felt.

"There's no getting around it," I told her. "The guy outfoxed us. Nobody expected a move like that, or Queenan would have had somebody in position to get hot on his trail."

"Now what?" Busic said. "We just wait to see if he holds up his end and lets the girl go?"

"I'm not that sure he will." I didn't like saying it out loud, but there it was. "The deal was no cops. But he obviously knew they were going to be there, or he could have skipped the Flying Wallendas act. Who knows what he'll do now? Hell, it could be that he never intended to let her go in the first place."

"What are you going to do now?"

"By *you*, do you mean me, or do you mean me and Queenan and his crew?"

Her voice lowered. "I mean *you*. She's your client. And you're a P.I., meaning you can work a little differently. Plus, you have a certain reputation in the department."

"Yeah, I'm plenty aware of my reputation."

"I'm not talking about that," she said. "I think you'd be surprised. So just between us, what *are* you going to do?"

I waited a little while before I answered. But my instincts told me I could trust her. "Well, I've got one good lead…"

"That Queenan doesn't know about?"

"I haven't told him. He wouldn't like how I got it."

"Then I don't need to know either. Just let me know how it turns out. And find the girl."

* * *

After my call, I told Queenan I was knocking off for the night.

"Yeah," he said, "I guess me and the boys might as well pack it in, too. We gotta face it—this shitbird led us a merry chase and done a nifty fade on us. Hell, we can't knock on every door in the city."

"Any of your guys who had a closer look able to say if this guy was Stuckey?"

"Nope. The picture we got is a few years old, and his hair's blond. Don't mean nothin', it'd be an easy fake. Add the glasses and the lip warmer, darken the hair…. Coulda been him or it coulda been John F. Doe. Anyhow, I'll get a bulletin out on Stuckey and one on an 'unknown suspect' just in case they ain't one and the same."

"Maybe we'll get lucky with the briefcase."

He shook his head. "Deacon's already got the lab boys on it. No prints—looks like it was wiped clean. And no labels in the coat or hat. We got zilch there."

"Damn. Pipe still in the coat pocket?"

"Nah. Took it with him, I guess, or pitched it. We ain't found it."

He took his stained hat off and scratched his scalp. "Anyway, it's been a long night. Head on home and grab some shuteye. Maybe we'll hear something by morning. If not, ring me up or drop by the barn and we'll see where we're at."

* * *

I drove back to my building to collect my dog and to trade cars back with Benjy. I could tell the kid was straining at the seams with questions, but he knew me well enough to save them. He also knew me well enough to know that I'd be starving.

"Here you go, Mr Ross." He handed me a paper bag as Monte and I headed for the diner door. "Meatloaf sandwich, on the house."

I could smell the aroma through the paper. I slapped him on the shoulder, "You're one in a million, kid."

* * *

On the drive over, I ate most of the sandwich and fed the rest to Monte. It was after eleven when I parked in front of the Singer house. I'd been a little hesitant about coming by that late—I knew Mrs. Singer's workday started early. But the living room lights were on, and behind the curtains I could see a dim shadow moving. It seemed to be someone pacing.

Monte groused a little when I told him to stay put. I went up the short walk and tapped on the door. It opened mid-knock.

"Mr. Ross, I've been trying to call you all evening," she snapped.

"I've been out and about," I said, with no attempt at an apology. She seemed to think my whole day was spent sitting by the phone.

She stepped back to let me in, and right off, I knew something was wrong. She seemed fidgety and agitated, and her hair was a tangled mess, like she'd been yanking at it. She was still in her work clothes but wearing house slippers. A smoking cigarette was in her hand, and a smoldering butt was on top of a small pile in an ashtray on the coffee table. A bottle and half a tumbler of bourbon sat next to it.

"What's the matter?" I asked when she had shut the door behind us. "Something up with Jimmy?" I looked around. "Did he come back home?"

"No, I haven't seen him since I talked to you. But I'm awfully worried." She looked it—her eyes were bouncing like ping pong balls, and her hands shook so much she was scattering ashes all over the worn carpet.

I eased her into her rocker and took a seat on the sofa across from her. I laid my hat next to the ashtray. "What's got you worried?"

She made a couple of false starts before she could get any words out. "I have a gun," she said at last. "A .38. Jimmy's father left it to me." Her eyes and tone went bitter. "About all he left me." She pulled a wadded handkerchief from her pocket and blew her nose loudly. "Anyway, it's missing. I keep it in a drawer in my bedroom, and I opened it earlier to get a pair of scissors and …it's gone. And I don't know how long it's been missing."

"Loaded?" I asked.

Her eyes went to the glass on the table, and I wondered if she thought I meant her. But the corners of her mouth twitched in a quick, mocking grin. "An unloaded gun isn't much use, is it?"

"Okay." I touched her arm. "It doesn't mean Jimmy's in any danger. His girl—his *wife*—has been kidnapped, and he's just a boy and doesn't know what to do. Maybe it makes him feel safer. Or maybe he's got some goofy kid notion that he's going to rescue her."

Her eyes stopped roaming the room and fixed on me. "You don't think he'd really try something?"

I couldn't hold back a laugh. "If the whole L.A.P.D. detective squad and yours truly can't find these people, no offense, but what chance has your son got? No, I think he's just a teenage boy who's probably read too many adventure stories, and having a gun makes him feel brave and tough and ready for whatever comes his way."

It didn't seem to comfort her much. She dropped the half-smoked cigarette on top of the rest and took a healthy dose of the whiskey. She closed her eyes and took a deep, deep breath, then focused on me.

"Will you find him for me? Before anything bad…" She let that hang. "I can't pay much, but—"

I stopped her with a hand. "My days are pretty full at the moment, looking for your new daughter-in-law, but I wouldn't worry much. I have a feeling that once we find her, or she turns up, Jimmy won't be far behind."

She nodded and chewed on that. She took another drink—a sip this time—and her brows came together with a new thought. "Why are you here?" she asked. "You didn't know I was calling, so why come at this hour? Hoping to see Jimmy, or…?"

"No," I said. "Not exactly. I mean, I hoped he'd be here because I had a question to ask him. But I'm guessing you can answer it for me. How does Jimmy know Roy Stuckey?"

Chapter Twenty-Four

I drove back to the office and sat down to scratch out some notes on everything Muriel Singer had told me before I forgot any of the details. I'd just gotten going when Monte made a peculiar, keening sound that I'd come to recognize, if not understand. I didn't know if he could feel a vibration in the wires, if there was some telltale noise only his ears could pick up, or if it was some mystical canine sixth sense. He didn't always do it, but every time he made that noise, the same thing happened seconds later.

"Were you sitting on the phone?" Vera Busic asked me. "How did you manage to answer before the first ring was done?"

"Secrets of the modern private investigator," I said. I noticed a tremor of excitement in her voice.

"I didn't really expect to catch you there," she said. "But I tried your house first. He called."

I sat up straighter. "Our kidnapper?"

"Yes. About fifteen minutes ago. Audrey's long in bed, but he gave me the message. He's letting her go."

I'd been so worn out when I got back to the office that I'd considered just spending the night there. Now I was wide awake. "What exactly did he say?"

"A lot of crap about how you can't trust a cop's word, and how he ought to just plant the girl out in the desert and so on. But I gave him the soft soap about what a neat trick he had pulled on you guys and how we'd underestimated him, etcetera. He laughed at that and said he was sharper than any hundred coppers." She snickered. "Of course, I didn't bother to point out that we already have a pretty good idea who he is, and that we sure as hell caught him the last time he was capering around."

"Where's the *letting her go* part?"

"You boys." She gave a quiet laugh. "Always in such a hurry. He says to be at the streetcar station at Western and Franklin after six tomorrow morning, and that we should watch for her on the outbound cars."

"Did he say which car? What time, I mean?"

"Unfortunately, he did not."

"Shit—sorry. That means we could be looking at any time from six to midnight."

"It's a good way to buy himself time," she said. "He keeps us busy watching the stop for who knows how long while he disappears with his sixty thousand dollars."

"Does Queenan know about this?"

"Yes. And if you think he's a grouch normally, try getting him out of bed."

"No thanks. Does Audrey know?"

"Not yet. I was going to wake her after I talked to you."

"Let her sleep. I'm sure she needs it. Anyway, we can't know for sure that this is on the level. This whole thing may be just a stall."

"How's that?"

"I wouldn't be surprised that the only person who comes in on the streetcar is another hired shill carrying a note telling us Beth is somewhere else. That would buy him even more getaway time. Or in the worst case, nobody shows on the car at all. Either way, I wouldn't want to get Audrey's hopes up just to have them cave in again."

"She's bound to find out in the morning."

"Yeah, but with any luck, we'll know more by then. Meanwhile, does anybody else know about the call?"

"No, Queenan sent all the boys home. He said I could man the phone as well as any of them." She gave a hard little laugh. "I guess I ought to be flattered."

"You're a damn good copper, sister. Don't let anybody tell you different."

"Thanks, Nate."

Chapter Twenty-Five

I was up and out well before the sun and went straight to the office. The diner wasn't open yet, but I knew Benjy came in early to do the books. I was able to cadge a donut and coffee, and a little dog sitting duty out of him.

Upstairs, I had some calls to make. Dusty, being an old cowboy, was always up with the roosters. Danny, on the other hand, was a night owl—I had to shag him out of the sack. He grumbled about it, but the promise of a C-note for some easy shadow work perked him up, and he said he'd throw his pants on and be right along.

I could always count on Aggie to be in her office plenty early. I had to wait while she gnawed my ear off over not clueing her in about the play at Angel's Flight. Of course, she'd already heard all about it, though she wasn't about to tell me how. But once she gave her viper tongue a rest, and I told her why I called, her tone turned to milk and honey.

Dusty and Danny showed up almost together, so I only had to explain about the call and run down my plan one time.

"I have my doubts," I told them, "But I need to copper my bet in case this guy's not just giving us the gas. If he does put the girl on the red car, we don't know where he'll do it. I'm sure Queenan's going to have all the stops covered, but I want you two to be at the Subway Terminal by six."

I showed both of them the photos that I had of Beth and Stuckey. "This bird," I said, holding up Stuckey's mug shot, "will probably be disguised. He may have dark hair and a mustache. Maybe glasses." I held up Beth's photo. "Just concentrate on the girl. Dusty, I want you on the car by six. Ride it all the way to Western and Franklin. Danny, you need to look sharp, and whoever the girl shows up with, you tail him wherever he goes. If he goes to ground, or especially if he shows any sign of taking a powder, call this number." I gave him a card with Vera Busic's name and Audrey's phone number written on it. "I'll be checking in with her for any news."

I pulled out my wallet and tossed him a bill. "There's your century in advance. If you need to take a cab, bus, train, or whatever to stay on this bird, pay for it out of that. I'll make up the difference later."

He pocketed the note. "Right-o, chief. I'll stick to him like fly paper."

"All right then, on your way, *muchacho*. I don't want you boys to show up together. This guy's a sharp operator." He saluted, and I watched him drift out.

I turned to Dusty. "Don't approach the girl if she comes on board. It's unlikely, but the guy may have someone watching her. He's not going to want her talking to anyone until he's made his clean sneak." I gave him the same name and phone number. "Anything screwy happens along the way, try to grab the girl and get her to safety, then call it in. You've got Sam Colt with you?"

He pulled his coat aside to show me the big stag-handled six-gun in his belt. "I'll look out for her, Nate. Don't you worry."

"I won't, but you look out for yourself, too. Walt will skin me alive if I let you get hurt."

He grinned under his big mustache. "Hell, I've chased bandits and cutthroats over half of—this ain't nothin'. I'm a pretty sharp operator myself."

Just as he stood to go, my phone rang. "Hold up a second," I told him as I grabbed up the receiver. "In case this is some news."

I listened to the caller, scribbled a note, said "Okay, thanks, very much," and hung up. I went to the bookshelf, pulled out a big, dog-eared volume, and flipped through it until I found what I was after.

"Change of plans," I told Dusty. "Let's go get Monte. You two are coming with me."

Chapter Twenty-Six

I filled Dusty in as we made the short drive east past Silver Lake.

"We've thought Roy Stuckey was our boy from pretty early on," I told him. "His partner from his old capers was the guy who got killed the other night."

"After the drop at the movie house."

"Right, the pickup man. Anyway, I got a look at Stuckey's file in Queenan's office. They were running a blackmail racket, and his file had photos of the demand notes they sent their marks. Handwritten notes." I pulled the note from Jimmy and Beth's little scheme from my pocket and handed it to Dusty.

He read it and looked a question at me. "Same handwriting," I said. "Doesn't take an expert to see it."

He thumped a finger on the note. "How's this Stuckey figure into this deal?"

"I talked to Jimmy Singer's mom. Stuckey's her son from her first marriage."

"Then was he part of the first ransom deal?"

"I don't really think he was. They only got two grand. Even if they cut him in for half, that's chump change." I pointed at the note. "But he obviously knew about it. I guess Jimmy figured if you need a ransom note, ask a pro. The mother didn't know about it, but she knew the kids were running off to Las Vegas. She'd overheard Jimmy telling Roy about it."

Dusty mulled that over. "Then Roy got ideas, and him and his buddy grabbed the girl for real, figuring they could get a whole lot more."

"That's how I see it. Maybe Stuckey didn't know who the girl was at first—or who her sister was—or maybe he did and was just biding his time."

"Makes sense, I guess." He looked around as we cruised down Silver Lake Blvd. "Now you want to tell me where is it we're headed?"

"The mother didn't know where Stuckey was living—he's a con trying to stay one jump ahead of his parole officer. But she found a note in Jimmy's room with Roy's name and a phone number. I looked it up in my reverse directory—it comes back to a house just a few blocks from here."

"Don't you think we ought to let Queenan know?"

"No time. This guy's ready to blow town, and now he's got plenty of scratch to do it. I figure by now either he's headed out to put the girl on the streetcar like he said, or he's holed up waiting to make his move. If she's already on the car, fine—we'll get her back all right. But if she's not, then he may have other plans. And if that's the case I don't like her odds."

* * *

The sun was just starting to throw a faint glow over the hills to the east as I turned right from Allesandro onto a block with only a couple of working streetlamps. I smiled and shook my head as I rounded the corner and my headlights raked the street sign. Only then did it hit me.

"What's funny?" Dusty asked.

"Oakglen Place," I said. "Binny Landis's last words. He wasn't telling me that they took Beth to *old Glenn's*, he was saying *Oakglen*."

He laughed softly. "Well, I'll be damned."

A worn-out two-story frame house sat on a small lot midway down the block. Its peeling clapboard front had the number I was looking for stenciled on one corner, but I saw four small mailboxes next to the recessed front door.

I swore under my breath as I pulled to the curb two houses past. "It's been split into apartments."

"And we don't know which one?"

"Nope." I cut the engine. "Wait here."

I got out, closed the door as quietly as I could, and walked back toward the house. I avoided the cracked walkway and instead cut across the small front lawn to the tiny front porch. Squinting in the feeble light from the overhead bulb, I could see the mailboxes had no names, only numbers. Tacked onto the front door was a small, faded card that read "Manager."

I drew my .380 and took off my hat, holding it over the hand with the gun in it. I tapped on the door and heard a muffled voice from behind say something I couldn't make out.

The door opened, and a pudgy, middle-aged man in baggy pants, a stained undershirt, and stocking feet blinked sleepy eyes at me. He had two empty milk bottles in one hand and scratched his stubbled chin with the other. He started to speak, but the words turned into a wet yawn. I had to wipe a little spray off my cheek.

"Sorry, bud," he said in a groggy voice. "I thought you were the milkman. Forgot to put these out." He looked at his watch and scowled. "But if you're here about the vacancy, have a heart and come back after breakfast."

"Not why I'm here." I pulled out the juice badge. I was going to have to lock the thing away—using it was becoming a bad habit. "I'm looking for a man who came in to report a lost Masonic ring. I'm damned if I can read the name he wrote down, but I made out the phone number all right." I showed him a slip of paper with the number Muriel Singer had given me.

"Hold on." He retreated and came back without the bottles, a pair of glasses on his nose. He peered at the note. "That's my number," he said. "Only phone in the place. I let the tenants use it for an extra buck a month. A guy, you say?"

"Right. Tall, thin, dark hair and a mustache." I pointed to his face. "Had glasses, if I recall. Anyway, I've got his ring for him."

"That sounds like Mr. Coletti in number three." He pointed straight up. "Italian fellow, lives with his sister. Poor girl's blind. Wouldn't have figured him for a Mason, though." He motioned behind him. "You want to go up?"

"I need to get my partner from the car first. And the ring, of course. Be right back."

He was waiting at the door wearing carpet slippers when I came back with Dusty and Monte in tow. He looked Dusty over from Stetson to boots and back.

"Pickpocket squad," I explained.

"Oh, right." He gave me a knowing look. "Is that a real police dog?"

"As real as they come."

He gave Monte a wide berth as he led us into what had started as a living room but had been converted into a small office. He opened a side door that connected to a short hallway. A door at the back end appeared to lead outside, and one on the right had a brass number two on it. A stairway led up to a landing with doors on either side.

"Three's up here on the left," the manager said. "Need me to go up with you?"

"That might be best," I said. "I wouldn't want to frighten the young lady." I looked at the back door. "Is there a back way out of their apartment?"

"Yep. There's a back door that leads to a set of stairs down to the yard." He gave me a cagey look. "Why does that matter?"

I pointed at Monte. "The dog. Just in case he has to…you know."

"Got it." He gave me a wink and motioned up the stairway. "Shall we?"

"You know what?" I said, stepping toward the back door. "Maybe I'd better let him take care of business now." I looked at Dusty. "Be right back." I slapped my leg. "Come on, boy."

Monte followed me down two brick steps into the small, fenced-in back yard. An alley ran behind the place, but I saw no cars parked there. A flight of wooden steps ran down the back wall at the west end. I walked Monte over to the bottom of the steps.

"Sit," I told him. He sat. I pointed up the stairs. "Watch." I walked back to the door, but before I went back in, I looked back at my furry pal. He was gazing up the stairs with an expectant dog smile, his tail gently working back and forth. He watched.

Manager in the lead, the three of us filed up the stairs. Dusty and I stood on either side of the door, tight against the wall, while the manager gave it a polite knock. No answer. Dusty and I looked at each other. The manager knocked again.

Inside, I heard a shuffling noise and the creak of a floorboard. A nasally voice called out, "Who it is-a, please?" in an accent that sounded no more

Italian than Chico Marx.

"Earl Platt," our companion answered. "The manager."

"One-a momenta," the fake Italian answered. More shuffling, a couple of footsteps, and the door opened six inches. "Si?" came the voice.

I tilted my head out just enough to see who spoke. The man was looking at the manager with irritation. Dark hair, dark mustache, and up close, no mistake. Definitely the acrobat from Angel's Flight, and definitely Roy Stuckey.

His eyes shifted to me and went wide, and his face disappeared from the doorway. I grabbed the manager's shoulder, yanked him out of the way, and hit the door with all my weight. It flew back, banged into something solid, and I heard something made of glass or china hit the floor and shatter as I plowed in, gun in hand, with Dusty right behind me. To my right, I heard scrambling feet and a door being yanked open. I ducked through an arched doorway into a narrow kitchen, and through the open back door I saw Stuckey vault over the low railing of the stair landing and drop down toward the yard below.

Before I reached the door, I heard a couple of quick barks, a feral snarl, and the soft scramble of feet on grass, followed by a long, unholy wail of pain. I came out onto the landing and, in the early morning light, saw Stuckey on hands and knees, furiously clawing at the grass, trying to get free while Monte held firm with his teeth sunk into the seat of his pants.

Chapter Twenty-Seven

"Good boy, Monte," I said to the big mutt as I pulled him off with one hand and held Stuckey at gunpoint with the other. Dusty moved in with the bracelets I'd brought along, and Stuckey yowled some more when Dusty pulled his arms back, handcuffed him, and yanked him to his feet.

"Whatta you want-a? You rob-a me?"

"Save it, pal. You're no more dago than I am." I tucked my .380 away and pulled out the mug shot. I held it up for him to see, and he spit at it.

He dragged his feet as we walked him to the staircase and planted them when we reached it. "Easy or hard, buddy," I told him. "Your choice. You can either walk up the stairs, or I can have my friend here drag you by your ass." I laid a hand on Monte's head. "Which will it be?"

He looked black murder at me, but allowed Dusty to guide him up the stairs without any more fuss. Halfway up, he tried to look over his shoulder at his backside. "Am I bleeding bad?" he asked, finally dropping the vaudeville accent.

"Not bad enough," Dusty answered.

Inside, Stuckey howled some more when Dusty pushed him down into a kitchen chair. He laid off it when I sat Monte three feet away and said, "Watch him, boy."

I looked at Dusty, and he jerked his chin toward the arched doorway. "Go on. This fellow ain't going nowhere."

I looked at Stuckey. "She'd better be all right." He started to say something, but bobbed his head up and down instead.

Off the other side of the living room was a hallway no more than ten feet long. In the middle was an open bathroom door, and there was a door at either end. One was open, and the coat hanging on a chair back and the stuff scattered on the night table told me that room was Stuckey's. The other door was closed and, when I tried it, locked. My first thought was to shoulder through it, but I didn't want to give the poor kid any more frights. I stepped into Stuckey's room and saw a key among the junk on the table. When I tried it on the locked door, it fit.

I opened the door as gently as I could. She was huddled in the corner farthest from the door, next to a window I could see had been nailed shut. She had to have heard all the ruckus and wondered whether it meant good or bad news for her. She was a petite girl, not quite as tall as Audrey but with the same white blonde hair. She looked in better shape than I'd imagined, considering her ordeal.

She looked at me with wide eyes as blue as Audrey's, and the knuckles of one fist pressed against her half-opened mouth.

I smiled at her. "Hello, Beth," I said in my softest voice. "My name's Nate. Your—Audrey—sent me. It's time to go home."

She didn't say anything, just stared at me without blinking. The eyes grew even wider and started to fill with tears.

I went back to the kitchen, being sure to leave her door open. Dusty had laid down a damp towel for Stuckey to rest his punctured posterior on. It was all the first aid he was going to get. Dusty gave me a questioning glance, and I nodded and mouthed a silent "She's okay." I drew a glass of water and took it back in to Beth.

She looked calmer as she sat on the bed and sipped gratefully at the water, while I took a quick look around the room. There wasn't much to see. Beth's few clothes were hanging in a tiny closet, and her other things were tucked away in a little two-drawer chest.

On top of the chest, I found a curly black wig and a pair of tortoise shell sunglasses with extra dark lenses. I picked them up for a closer look and saw that the lenses had been painted black on the insides.

"They made me wear those," she said in a steadier voice than I would have expected. "Anytime we went out. So that I couldn't tell where we were." She pointed to the closet. "There's a white cane in there. I had to carry it to make people think I was blind."

I took a deep breath. There was no easy way to ask. "Beth, did they hurt you? In any way at all?"

She met the question with a level gaze, and I was struck again with how much she looked like Audrey. "No," she said at last. "They treated me okay, mostly. They made all kinds of threats so that I'd do what they told me to do, but they never touched me." She sipped more water and looked at me with her head tipped a little to one side. "Are you a policeman, Nate?"

"I used to be," I told her. "I'm a private investigator. Audrey hired me to find you."

"Took you long enough." There wasn't a trace of bitterness in the remark. She looked at me over the rim of the glass as she drank, and I could see the beginnings of a smile. I liked the kid.

I didn't want to waste any more time going through the place. The cops would have to do it when they got here anyway. "You mind coming downstairs with me for a minute, Beth? I need to make a phone call or two."

She set the glass down and stood up. "No, it'll be nice to get out of here." She looked at the wig and glasses. "Especially without those on."

As we walked through the living room, she glanced toward the kitchen doorway. She paled a little when she spotted Stuckey sitting there with Dusty hovering over him. Stuckey was looking at the floor, and if he saw her, he didn't show it. She gave Dusty a curious look; he smiled at her and tipped his hat.

"Don't let that big mustache fool you," I told her. "He's one of the good guys. He's with me."

* * *

We went downstairs and through the connecting door into the manager's apartment. We found him at the table in a small kitchen, eating a bowl of cereal. He looked up and seemed confused when he saw Beth, then he gave me a dark look and wiped milk off his lip with a thumb.

"Mason's ring, my eye."

"Sorry about that, Mr. Platt. But cheer up—your little apartment building's about to get some primo publicity. You won't have any trouble filling that vacancy now." His face went blank, and before he could ask, I said, "I need to use your phone."

It took some time, and more than one phone call back and forth, to get all the right people informed and to call off the dogs. I gave Busic the information, and she passed it on to Queenan when he checked in. Queenan, in turn, sent patrol coppers to us to take Stuckey off our hands. First, they'd take him to the receiving hospital to get Monte's handiwork cleaned and stitched, and then he'd be off to booking.

Queenan also sent Deacon and Valverde to take charge of the apartment and to wait for the lab boys. He notified Audrey, who was anxiously waiting with Spencer at the streetcar stop, that Beth was safe and unharmed. He got word to Aggie, who was also waiting at the stop for the scoop I'd promised her. He even sent a couple of bluesuits to find Danny Isaac and tell him he'd just made the easiest hundred dollars of his life. Last of all, Queenan sent instructions via Busic for Dusty and me to take Beth straight to Audrey's estate. He told her he would meet us there and warned that there better not be "anymore cowboyin'" or he'd have both our scalps.

* * *

Beth sat up front with me while Dusty and Monte shared the back seat. I got the story from her as we drove to Audrey's. I didn't spend much time talking over hers and Jimmy's bonehead play. I told her up front that I already knew about it, and more importantly, that Audrey did. I was happy to see that she seemed properly mortified at that. Still, she filled in a detail or two for me that helped things make sense.

She told me that after Las Vegas, they'd checked into the hotel near Echo Park. She was afraid to leave the room—worried about being spotted. Jimmy would go out for anything they needed. Meanwhile, they talked about how to break the news to Audrey. Beth said she wanted visit "Uncle Griffin" and borrow money to pay Audrey back, but Jimmy insisted on going to straight to Audrey.

"He said it was the only right thing. It was our first fight," she said with a sniffle.

I told her for what it was worth that it wouldn't be their last. That got a little smile.

While Jimmy was gone one day, she went on, two men came to the door posing as police officers. She was afraid they'd come because of the ransom note, so she let them in. She started to get suspicious when they told her they needed to take her in for questioning but refused to wait for Jimmy or even to let her leave a note for him.

When she flat-out refused to go with them, they grabbed her by the arms, and she struggled. They told her that if she fought or screamed, they were going to wait until Jimmy came back and kill him. Then she gave in, got into a car with them, and they made her lie down on the back seat so she couldn't see where they were headed. The two men, who she said called each other Sam and Joe, took her to a rooming house—the description she gave fit Binny Landis's dump—and held her there for a day or two. They took her out one of the days wearing the wig and blindfold glasses. She couldn't tell where they went; she only heard street noises, but they'd let her talk to Audrey on the telephone. Another day, they went to Union Station—she couldn't see, but she could tell by the sounds she heard. Again, they'd let her speak on the phone with Audrey.

After that, she said, they'd taken her to the place where we found her. She said that Joe didn't come around anymore. I didn't tell her about Landis's death or the stolen ransom. Plenty of time for her to learn about those things later. She said Sam had left her tied up in the house on Oakglen while he went to make the last ransom call to Audrey.

She said that other than the weak tussle in the hotel, the two men had never roughed her up or touched her, except to lead her by the arm when they were out in public. They threatened to kill her if she made trouble or tried to escape, but otherwise, she said, they'd left her alone.

* * *

I noticed unusual traffic on the normally quiet private road as we wound our way up toward Audrey's. When the gate came in sight, I saw a handful of cars parked haphazardly on either side and across the road. A cluster of about two dozen people on foot milled around the gate. When we got closer, I spotted the big, boxy cameras and knew it was a flock of newshawks. Nothing stays quiet in this burg for long.

Two uniformed officers stood sentry duty at the gate, keeping the unhappy reporters and photographers at bay. The coppers parted the buzzing crowd to allow us in, and I was almost blinded by a salvo of popping flash bulbs as we passed through. When we approached the house, the first thing I noticed was Queenan, pacing the big veranda out front. I could see he was fuming. I expected no less. I parked under the canopy, and he tossed his cigar and started stalking our way, but before he could get a word out, the huge front door swung open, and Audrey came charging out.

She bore straight for my car, and as Beth climbed out wrapped her in her arms. The two of them stood there for five full minutes, hugging, weeping, laughing, and weeping some more, while the rest of us just stood watching without a word.

Spencer and Mrs. Borne came out of the house and stood at a respectful distance. Mrs. Borne was crying pretty freely, and Spencer's upper lip seemed to have lost a little of its usual stiffness. When the two Chase women broke their clinch, Beth went over to them, gave each one a quick hug, and exchanged a few warm words.

Not far behind Audrey, I saw Aggie Underwood sidle out the front door, notebook at her side, and give a few quiet directions to the photographer who trailed her. She gave me a wink when she looked my way, and as the camera jockey was shooting Audrey and Beth, I saw even my hard-nosed reporter pal thumb away a tear or two.

Audrey watched Beth talking with the two staff members with glowing eyes and palms together in front of her face. She wiped her eyes and looked around, and when she saw me standing by the car, she rushed my way. She seized my hands in both of hers and her eyes bored into mine for what seemed like an eternity.

"Thank you, Nate," she said. Her voice was heavy and choked with emotion. "I don't know how I can ever thank you enough." Before I could say a word, she threw her arms around me, pressed her face against my chest, and started in weeping again. Between bouts of crying and gasping for breath, she whispered, "Thank you," over and over again.

I put my arms around her shoulders and made what I hoped were comforting noises. I understood her emotion, but I felt like a sap with her pouring it out on me like that in full view of God, Queenan, and everybody. I looked around to see Queenan smirking and Aggie giving me a sort of proud, motherly look. The worst was her photographer, who aimed his big Speed Graphic at us and captured the whole scene for posterity. If I'd had my hands free, I would have ripped it out of his mitts and beaned him with it.

The happy reunion concluded, Audrey took Beth inside, followed by Aggie, the camera guy, and Mrs. Borne. Dusty chatted with Spencer next to my car. Spencer watched the group go in, then excused himself and came over to me. He pulled off a glove and extended a hand.

"Well done, Mr. Ross," he said in his usual clipped, emotionless way. "Very well done, sir."

"Thanks, Spencer." We shook, and he put his glove back on, turned on his heel without another word, and went into the house to join the others.

"*Very well done, sir,*" Queenan said in a mimicking voice. His British accent was worse than Stuckey's Italian. He drilled me with a hard eye. "If you're all through takin' bows and signin' autographs and gettin' slobbered on by movie queens, you and me need to have some words."

I asked Dusty to go in with the rest and wait for me. He looked at Monte, who poked his big, shaggy head out the side window. "What about this old scamp?"

"Take him in with you," I told him. "He's got a standing invitation."

* * *

I followed Queenan down the long, graveled drive in the direction of the cottage. He ambled along two steps ahead of me, hands behind his back, trailing smoke over his shoulder like a locomotive. I knew he was building up a head of steam.

When we'd walked fifty yards or more and were well out of earshot of the house, Queenan stopped. He turned, half facing me, half looking out over the wide green.

"This was supposed to be a partnership deal, remember? Fifty-fifty. I'm sure you was no happier about it than me, but I had orders. And now I've got to go to the Chief of Police, hat in hand, and explain to him how a private badge beat us out on the biggest case to come down the pike in a while. You think I'm lookin' forward to that, Ross?"

He turned to look full at me. "I told you I couldn't afford no cowboyin' on this thing, and what do you do first chance you get? You hold out on me, then you saddle up and ride hell for leather, you and your rope-spinnin' pal, and leave me and my boys chokin' on your dust."

"It wasn't like that, Cap," I said. "I didn't hold out on you. Singer's mother called me early in the morning because she had found Stuckey's phone number. I matched it to an address, and Dusty and I just went to see if it panned out. I would have called you out, but things moved too fast."

At least some of that was true. He chewed his cigar and stared at me. Behind those angry eyes, I could hear the cogs and gears at work.

"Singer's mother," he said in a quiet voice, and I knew then that I'd flubbed it. "And just how and why would she have a phone number for a guy like Stuckey?"

"Okay, listen," I said. "I know how this is gonna look, but I wasn't trying to play a lone hand here. I was doing just what you told me I should, trying to find Jimmy Singer."

"And…"

"And it turns out that he and Stuckey are brothers. Well, half brothers—the mother's first marriage."

The red started rising in his face, and I tried to cut in before it reached his hairline. "I only found that out late last night. I was going to fill you in this morning, but…"

"Blah." He waved a hand like he was shooing away flies. "That means the Singer kid's mixed up in this kidnap business? The real kidnap?"

"No, but Stuckey knew about Jimmy and Beth's little grift." I left out that it was Stuckey who wrote the note—I didn't want to explain *how* I knew. "I guess it gave him some ideas."

He shook his big head. "Damn stupid kids. No idea the avalanche of crap they were about to bring down." He was about to say more, but something behind me caught his attention. I turned to see Decker double-timing our way.

"Hey, Cap," he said when he was near enough. "Thought you'd want to know I just heard from the boys at the gate, Jimmy Singer just showed up in a cab. He's on his way to the big house now."

Queenan grinned at me. "Well, speak of the devil, huh?" He turned back to Decker. "Thanks, Clyde." Decker about-faced and headed back at a brisk walk, and we followed, lagging several paces behind. As we walked, Queenan looked sidelong at me and chuckled.

"What's the joke, Cap?"

"You are," he said. "Some detective. You've been lookin' for this kid for days and couldn't find him, and now he finds you. Aggie Underwood should include *that* in her story."

* * *

Queenan and I walked into a celebratory scene. The whole party had crowded into the living room and made it look not as spacious. The French windows had all been thrown open to let in the fresh air.

Decker was already there along with Valverde and Deacon. Vera Busic stood with them, looking very different out of uniform, at one end of the room. At the other end, Monte sat next to Dusty, who made animated conversation with Spencer and Mrs. Borne. In the center, Beth and Jimmy sat together on the sofa, holding hands and smiling while Aggie talked to them and scribbled in her notebook, and directed her photographer as he got set to shoot the two newlyweds. Minus the two kids and my dog, everyone—even the coppers—was smiling over a glass of champagne.

I looked around for Audrey just as she came through a doorway carrying a tray with some glasses and a fresh bottle. Mrs. Borne tried to take charge of it, but Audrey waved her off. She spotted Queenan and me and glided over, beaming, to fix us up with champagne.

"Can we talk?" she said to me quietly while Queenan was draining his glass at a gulp. She set the tray down on a side table, and I followed her out through the French windows.

We walked side by side through the rose garden. When we reached the bougainvillea arbor, she took my hand, and we stopped.

"There is no possible way—there are no words, Nate—to tell you just how grateful I am for what you've done for me."

"You've already thanked me, Audrey. There's no need—"

"But there is. I could thank you all day, every day, for the rest of my life, and it wouldn't be enough."

"All I did was what you hired me to do."

She flinched like something had stung her. Her hand relaxed a bit in mine, but she still held on. "Speaking of which," she said in a flat voice, "I suppose we need to discuss your fee."

"Nothing to discuss. You paid me twenty five hundred dollars at the start. That more than covers it. Besides," I added, "the job's not quite done."

That seemed to shake her out of her momentary blues. "What do you mean? Beth's home, she's safe."

"Sure. And no mistake, that's the most important thing. But you're still out $30,000." Queenan's guys had found the final ransom payment stashed in Stuckey's room, but no sign of the first.

"I don't care about the money. I'd have paid a hundred times that to have my daughter back."

"I'm sure you would have. But let's not forget, a man was murdered for that money. Not a good man, I'll grant you, but murder's murder."

"Aren't the police investigating that?"

"They are. But as long as it's connected to Beth's kidnapping, it's part of my job, too. I can't just let it dangle. I don't like loose ends."

"How will you go about it?"

"I've got an idea or two. I'll know soon enough if they pay off."

She nodded and looked away. I could feel her drifting off, deep in thought. After a time, she looked back at me and smiled, but I didn't read any happiness in it.

"I suppose we should get back to the house," she said. "Aggie has more questions now that… Jimmy's here."

"What about Jimmy?"

She laughed. "Yes, what *about* Jimmy? Beth and I will need to have some long talks before we decide what about Jimmy."

"I hope you don't mind that I called Aggie. I knew the press hounds would be all over you when word got out that Beth was back. I thought if Aggie could get the story first, maybe it would hold off the feeding frenzy."

"No, she's been very kind and understanding from the first."

"Aggie's all right. A little rough around the edges, but solid gold inside."

"She's nothing like the Hollywood muckrakers I'm used to dealing with." She looked up at me and squeezed my hand tighter. "Thank you for her, too."

As we came closer to the house, I slipped my hand from hers. It wasn't that I gave a damn who saw us, or what they might make of it. They'd already seen plenty. It was a sudden feeling that if I didn't let go of that hand then, that I might never want to let go of it again.

* * *

The celebration broke up, and we all began going our separate ways. Spencer and Mrs. Borne went back to their duties. Jimmy left in a taxi, and I wondered if he'd be coming back or if Beth would be moving out. One of the many things she and Audrey had to work out, I supposed.

Queenan and his cops went back to the station to write reports and fill out forms, and handle all the nitty-gritty details involved in closing out the Elizabeth Chase kidnapping case. Whatever Queenan said, I couldn't see his chief giving him too much of an ass-chewing. Not all kidnappings, or celebrity capers for that matter, had such happy endings. However the story was told, the L.A.P.D. was going to end up looking pretty good.

Aggie and her cohort packed up their toys and made ready to head back to the newspaper office and get their scoop out before the other papers beat them to the draw. I'd scored big brownie points with her on this one, so she didn't bite my head off when I gave her a suggestion or two about the story.

Audrey threatened to turn on the weeps again when Dusty and I got ready to leave. I told her I'd keep her informed on the other matter, and she said she'd look forward to hearing from me. I loaded Monte in the car with Dusty and the three of us drove off and left Audrey and Beth to get properly caught up, and to start those long discussions.

* * *

I dropped Dusty at the Buscadero, then stuck around long enough to eat. Dusty told Pooter all about our morning's adventures over beer and what were now officially known as Busky Burgers.

When I pulled into the little parking lot to my building, I hadn't even set the handbrake when Benjy burst out of the diner and half sprinted to meet me.

"Captain Queenan called here looking for you," he panted. "About fifteen minutes ago. He's been trying your office. He said to have you call him p.d.q. He didn't say why, but it sounded pretty serious."

"Okay, pal, thanks."

Queenan wasn't in his office, and it took me two calls and two or three transfers before I got him.

"Ross—about damn time you called."

I pulled the receiver back from my ear. I'd forgotten how loud he could be on the telephone, even when he wasn't in a lather. I could tell right off something big was up.

"What's going on, Cap?"

"Your little pal, the perpetually missin' Jimmy Singer, just put in his second appearance today."

I had a bad feeling. "Where?"

"Right next door, at the receiving hospital. He just shot Roy Stuckey."

"What the hell?"

"Doctors had just finished sewin' up Stuckey's boo boo, and a couple of uniforms were takin' him off to jail. They were just loadin' him in the prowler to drive him over to Lincoln Heights when the kid comes walkin' up bold as brass, and pulls a .38. He says, 'Take that, you kidnappin' son of a bitch' or something along those lines, and he feeds Stuckey the dose. Four shots."

"Did he kill him?"

"Deader than silent movies."

"What about Jimmy?"

He snorted. "Get this. The little shitbird does his Billy the Kid bit, and before the patrol coppers can even break leather, he lays the gun down on the ground and grabs sky."

"Where is he now?"

"Got him in the tank downstairs. We gotta book him on murder, of course. But considerin' the circumstances and his tender years, I doubt the D.A.'s gonna come down too heavy, if he charges him at all. He's more likely to give him a medal."

"Can I talk to him?"

He gave a harsh laugh. "You've been workin' my goodwill pretty damn hard of late." He drew in a deep breath, blew it out again. "I hadn't oughta, but come on down—I'll give you a few minutes."

I called Benjy, and he promised to look in on Monte.

* * *

I couldn't figure it. Beth was back safe, the guys hadn't harmed her—physically anyway. Stuckey was a dead-bang cinch to spend the rest of his life in prison. Killing him was only going to spare him the monotonous hell of Folsom or San Quentin. Why give him that break?

It was just the latest question in a tangled mess of a case that left me more questions than answers. Who killed Griffin Glenn and why? Who tipped off the press about the kidnap, and again, why? Who killed Binny Landis? The *why* there seemed obvious, but where was the money? And why had Jimmy Singer, with his bride kidnapped, kept himself out of circulation for most of the week? Afraid of being the next kidnap victim? Running around playing junior G-man, trying to find his wife? The gun made sense in either case.

I sorted through everything I'd seen and heard and been told since this affair had started and couldn't come up with a single sensible answer to any one of those questions. Then I recalled something Beth had told me on the drive to Audrey's. And all at once the tumblers lined up, the latch clicked, and I was sure I'd unlocked the answers to all of them.

* * *

I had a quick talk with Queenan in his office and told him what I suspected. He was skeptical at first, but the more I talked, the less he scoffed and smirked and threw his "Blah" at me. In the end, he called Decker in and told him what he wanted done.

Jimmy was in one of the station's tanks—the bare, windowless, cheerless rooms where suspects were left to meditate on their sins before being interrogated, many times to the musical accompaniment of a little blackjack percussion.

Jimmy wasn't cuffed. The door was locked from the outside, so there was little need. He'd been made as comfortable as anybody ever was in those rooms. A paper cup of coffee with cream in it and a half-eaten cheese sandwich lay at his elbow on the scarred table. He rested his forearms on the tabletop with a tin ashtray between them and a nearly finished cigarette burning between his fingers. I hadn't known the kid smoked.

He looked up as I stepped into the room, and the door closed and locked behind me. His face was tired—as tired as an eighteen-year-old face can ever look—but he didn't appear to be nervous or scared. He gave me a lop-sided half smile as I sat across from him.

"Hey, Mr. Ross. Guess I got myself in quite a jam here, huh?"

"I'll say you did, pal."

"Does Beth know?"

"I couldn't tell you. I came straight here as soon as I heard."

He nodded, took a last drag off his butt, and stubbed it out in the ashtray. He dusted his fingers on his pant leg and stared at the table.

"Anything you need, kid?" I asked.

He shrugged. "A lawyer, I guess." His head came up, and he looked at the three-foot by four-foot mirror on the side wall. He flashed me a weak grin. "That's a one-way glass, right? Like in the movies. They're watching and listening, aren't they?"

I glanced at the mirror. "I don't know. Probably."

The grin widened. "Did they send you in here to talk to me? You know, friendly face, ask questions, get me to loosen up and tell you why I killed him?"

"No, Jimmy, I'm here on my own. And I've only got two questions for you."

He turned palms up on the table. "Okay, go ahead and ask 'em."

"First question—what makes you think I'm a friendly face?"

The kid was good. His face didn't give anything away, but there was a quick flicker in the eyes. The eyes did it every time.

"And what's the other question?" He tried to sound casual but couldn't quite pull it off.

"Why *did* you kill him?"

He blinked and jerked his head back a few inches. "Isn't it obvious? For what he did to Beth. For taking her and—"

I held a hand up to stop him. "I'm not talking about your brother Roy, Jimmy. I'm talking about Griffin Glenn."

His mouth dropped open a little, but he caught himself and turned it into a contemptuous smile. "What? You must be cracked in the head."

"I'm betting you didn't know the golden goose was flat broke. I'm betting you still don't know it."

He was straining to keep up his front, but I could see that that rocked him. Little beads of sweat showed in his hairline and on his upper lip.

I went on. "Beth loved the guy, and she believed him when he told her she'd have his fortune when his day finally came. She didn't know he was a drunken bum, and there was no fortune to leave behind—nothing but a lot of bad debt. And you believed Beth and knew that once the two of you were one, what *she* inherited, *you* inherited. But why wait when you could just make Griffin's day come a little early, am I right?

He glared at me, and his breathing started coming in bursts like he'd just finished a half-mile sprint. He shifted his eyes to the mirror and then back to me.

"No wonder you argued with Beth over going to visit Glenn," I said. "You didn't care about doing the 'only right thing'. You didn't want her getting wise to what you'd done."

"That's all bullshit," he said through clenched teeth.

"Sure it is. I guess it's also bullshit that you were the one who tipped the press when Beth got snatched for real. Did you know right off it was Roy, or did you only suspect it? Wait—sorry, I said only two questions. It doesn't matter anyway. You knew for sure when you saw his old partner, Binny Landis, make the pickup. Did you follow him, or did you know where he was staying and get there first? Damn it, there I go again—another question."

I let him chew on that while I lit a cigarette of my own." Anyway, you knock Binny off and score yourself an easy thirty grand. No need to wait for probate on Griffin Glenn's will now, plus if either murder goes sour on you, you've got a nice getaway stake. And I'm guessing—just guessing, mind you—that Roy knew about Griffin Glenn. That that's why you scratched him—it was nothing to do with what he did to Beth."

"Is this what they pay private eyes for?" The kid sneered. "To dream up a bunch of fairy tales?"

"No, Jimmy, they don't. See, fairy tales have happy endings. But you aren't going to get one of those. Because while you and I are talking here, the cops are checking the gun you shot your lowlife brother with to see if it's the one that killed Binny Landis. They're also at your mother's house searching your room for thirty thousand dollars."

That broke his tough guy act. His face went dead white, and his hands and legs started to shake.

"Maybe you'll get a free pass on Griffin Glenn—we'll see when they check your prints against what they found at his house. Either way, you're a done deal on the other two. And sonny, you just turned eighteen, which means we aren't talking about lockup here, we're talking about the gas." I stood up and walked to the door. I was about to knock to be let out, but paused and turned. "How about being a pal and allowing me just one more question before I go? Did you ever give a damn about Beth, or was she just supposed to be your ticket to the good life?"

He tried to hit me with a hard stare, but didn't have it left in him. His lip began to quiver, and tears started spilling down his cheeks. Instead of answering my question, he treated me to a string of names and slurs that might have caused me to leave an older guy short a few teeth.

"Look on the bright side, junior," I said as I gave the door two short raps. "Three murders, but they can only kill you once."

Chapter Twenty-Eight

Queenan dropped by the office after breakfast the next morning. He had a copy of the *Herald* under his arm and a more suspicious than usual look in his eye.

"Top of the morning, Cap," I said, beating him to his usual greeting.

"Ross," was his curt reply. He deposited his big frame in his customary chair, and the creak woke Monte, who'd been enjoying his mid-morning snooze. He looked at Queenan and gave a gentle thump of his tail, then went back to his nap.

"Looks like you two really are becoming pals," I said.

He brushed the comment away with a big mitt. "Let's just call it a truce." He unfolded the *Herald* with a flip of his wrist and laid it on the desk in front of me. "Seen this?"

I had, but I pretended to scan it with interest. The headline read *ELIZABETH CHASE RESCUED, KIDNAPPER ARRESTED* over the subhead *Sister of Movie Star Safe after Frightening Ordeal.* The byline read *by Agness Underwood.* The two-column piece underneath outlined, in Aggie's detailed and colorful style, how an able and dedicated team of detectives under the leadership of L.A.P.D. Homicide Captain Carl N. Queenan managed to locate the missing girl and bring her back unharmed. Not only that, but also to arrest the culprit and recover the sixty thousand dollars cash that Audrey Chase had paid in ransom.

I looked up from the paper. "What's the 'N' stand for?"

"None of your concern is what it stands for. And *that's* all you got to say?" He grabbed the paper and jabbed at the article with a sausage finger. "How much of this story's your doin'?"

"My doing? I didn't even see my name mentioned there."

"Exactly. That's my point."

I held my hands up in mock innocence. "I can't be responsible for what the press chooses to write. I'm just a lowly working stiff."

"You're full of shit, is what you are." He leaned back and glowered at me, but I could tell it was for show. He pulled out a cigar, trimmed it, and struck a match. "I swear, Ross. Every time I think I've got you figured, you up and surprise me."

"You're welcome, Cap."

He eyeballed me over the cigar as he lit it. "You didn't hear me say thanks."

"I'm pretty sure I did."

"Blah!" He shook the match out and tossed it at the ashtray on my desk. He missed by two inches.

I picked up the charred match and dropped it in the ashtray. "Don't tell me you came all the way over here just to read me the morning news."

He took a full puff, fogged the office. "Nah, I figured I'd give you the latest dope on young Mr. Singer in person."

"Don't tell me he's killed somebody else now."

"Funny you should say that. Jailer makin' his rounds last night found him standin' on his bunk, shirt off, one sleeve tied around his neck and the other tied around the ceiling light. Our boy was gettin' ready to do the last dance."

"No kidding? I can't say I'd have been sorry."

"You and me both, pal. For now, he's in one of the DT cells, padded walls and all. We got him buckled up in a cuckoo corset—he won't be pulling no more tricks."

"How are you boys coming on the cases?"

He grinned. "It gives me a pain where I sit to ever admit you was right, but we found the thirty big ones, minus sixty bucks, in the kid's room."

"Footlocker under the bed?"

"Nah, hidden in the lining of his letter jacket, hangin' in the closet."

"What about Glenn's house? Fingerprints?"

"Don't get greedy." He sighed. "Yeah, you was right there, too. We got

Singer's prints all over Glenn's house, includin' on that upstairs door frame and the railing."

"Is it enough to hang that one on him, too?"

His eyes twinkled, and he waggled his cigar. "It is now. That's the cherry I was savin'. The kid confessed."

"To everything?"

"The whole megillah. Cocky, braggin' about it all. Wants us to think he's Dillinger, Pretty Boy Floyd, and Baby Face Nelson all rolled into one." He laughed. "Don't know if he's heard how it went for those birds."

"Has the little bastard even asked after Beth?"

"Not a word. He's got some choice words for *you*, though."

"Yeah, he gave me all of 'em all in one breath. But back to Beth, how's she doing?"

"Busic spent another night, just to give the ladies a little peace of mind. I've been too busy catalogin' all of Singer's misdeeds to get out there and check on 'em." He studied the lit end of this cigar and blew on it to even the burn. "I kinda figured you might want to handle that end of things."

Before I could answer that, he held his palms out and stood up. "Don't get your temperature up—I ain't makin' any accusations." He moved to the door. "But I will say this, one guy to another. Audrey Chase? A man couldn't do no better than that, Ross." Hand on the doorknob, he took a look around the office. "But by God, *she* could, though."

Chapter Twenty-Nine

It took me a full day to convince myself. And my mind wasn't much on my driving as I snaked my way once more up the private road to Audrey Chase's estate. I took a couple of turns wide and nearly went off the road. I'd called ahead, and Spencer stood waiting for me and opened the gate. We exchanged quick pleasantries, and I drove on up to the house.

I was surprised when Audrey herself answered the door. Until then, I'd only seen her in casual, everyday clothes. Though even simply dressed, she was still a stunner, she really hadn't looked like a movie star. But today she was decked out in a glittery silver gown that fit her like a snakeskin. Clusters of diamonds around her neck and dangling from her ears caught the afternoon sun and flashed fire. Her pale hair was freshly set and hung in loose, shiny waves over her shoulders, and her mouth was painted a dark red that brought out the sparkle and intensity of her deep blue eyes. I'd found coherent speech a struggle the first time I met her, but seeing her like this, at first I couldn't speak at all. I just stood and stared. This wasn't going to make my job any easier.

"Hello, Nate." The warm smile was dazzling, but it was also familiar by now, and I felt my senses returning.

"Hello, Audrey. You look, uh…" My brain was functioning, but I couldn't come up with a word that was halfway adequate. "You look great." Sap.

"Thank you. I have to go to the studio later." She rolled her eyes. "Publicity photos." She smiled again, stepped back, and opened the door wider. "I'm sorry—won't you come in?"

"No Mrs. Borne today?" I asked as I followed her to the living room.

"She's upstairs, helping Beth." She waved me to the sofa, and I took a seat. Without asking, she went to a sideboard and poured us a couple of bourbons. She passed me my drink and sat gingerly on the edge of a chair. It looked a little uncomfortable—her dress wasn't made for sitting as much as for looking at.

"How is Beth?" I asked when she had settled.

"She's doing surprisingly well. Moving back into the house—that's what Mrs. Borne's helping her with. Of course, Griffin's death hit her especially hard. But if there's a blessing in it, it's that it made all the news about Jimmy much easier for her to accept. I'd worried that she might be broken-hearted over him—you know how foolish girls in love can be. But she hasn't shown much regret." She paused to take a sip of her bourbon, then grinned. "To be honest, I think after a few days with him, the luster was wearing off. Maybe she was starting to sense that he wasn't exactly what he seemed."

"And how are you?"

"Tired. Tired from worry and the stress. Tired of wondering, hoping, praying. Just tired."

I couldn't think of a proper response, so I changed the subject. "Queenan told me what you're planning. That after Jimmy's trial, you're letting Mrs. Singer keep the thirty thousand dollars."

"That poor woman," she said. "None of this was her doing. But to lose both her sons this way…awful. I wanted to do something. It's really not very much, considering."

"Maybe it's not much," I said, "But it's not nothing. It's very decent of you."

She seemed a little uneasy talking about Muriel Singer, so I switched topics again. I brought her up to date on the cases against Jimmy, and she told me how things were better now between her and Beth than they had ever been.

"It's strange," she said, "how something good can come out of so much tragedy."

"Life's peculiar that way."

We seemed to be running short of things to talk about and sat sipping our drinks in silence. After a couple of minutes of that, she leaned forward.

"Tell me something, Nate. Honestly. You spoke to Jimmy Singer—do you think he ever had any feelings at all for Beth?"

I'd been hoping she wouldn't ask me that. I cared too much to lie to her, but I was almost sure the answer wasn't going to give her any peace. I stalled with my drink while I tried to frame an easy reply. Finally, I just gave her what she asked for—honesty.

"I can't help believing that he was never anything but a schemer from the start, and that if he'd gotten away with things and life had gone on as they planned, one day he might have decided that Beth was dispensable too. I think she had a lucky escape."

She didn't say anything at first, just parted her lips in a little gasp and looked at me with those cobalt eyes. When she spoke, her voice was low and sad. "You live in a very bleak world, Nate."

"We all live in the same world, Audrey. Isn't that what our jobs are about—yours and mine? Trying in our own ways to make it a little less bleak?"

She looked at me for a long moment. "Yes, I suppose you're right."

We spent a few more minutes trying to lighten the mood with meaningless small talk. When it ran dry, I told her that I knew she needed to head off to the studio soon and that I needed to get back and check on Monte.

"Where is Monte today?" she asked.

"I left him at the office. He's in charge when I'm gone. He's cheaper than a secretary, and he only takes five-minute lunches."

She laughed at that, and I was happy to see some of the light come back into her eyes. She walked me to the door, and when we got there, she stopped and turned to face me.

"I'm so very grateful for all you've done, Nate. Not just for Beth, but for… I'm actually far more than grateful."

"Audrey, you don't have to—"

She stopped me with a hand on my chest. "I wouldn't want you to think… That is, I don't want to be forward, but…but now that this terrible thing is behind us, could we possibly…"

I took hold of her other hand. She was staring into my eyes, and I felt my resolve starting to crumble, but I knew I had to get the words out.

"Audrey, I'm flattered. I am. Let's be honest, any man with blood in his veins would be. But we're just not…" I wracked my brain for the right phrase.

"Is it because of what I do? All the silly attention, the newspapers, the stupid…" She waved a hand at her dress. "…publicity?"

"No, it's not any of that." I turned her hand loose and touched her cheek. "Give me that much credit—my ego's not that fragile."

"Then what is it?"

"You and I are from two different worlds, kid."

"But you just said we live in the same world."

"You're right, I did. I guess what I mean is the same world, but two completely different realms, if that makes any sense. You live in the limelight, and I live in the dark. I'm not meant for the limelight, and I wouldn't for all the world drag you into the darkness. If I did, sooner or later we'd both be sorry."

I could see that wherever her heart was, her head was telling her I was right. The pleading look in her eyes changed to understanding, then resignation. She nodded once, dropped her hand from my chest, and opened the door.

As I stepped past her, she grabbed my arm, and when I turned, she stepped in and kissed me. We stood for half a minute or more, our foreheads touching, and then I took a step back.

"Goodbye, Nate," she said.

"Goodbye, Audrey."

Chapter Thirty

A week later, an envelope came in with the morning's mail. Heavy stationery—quality, cream-colored stuff, not the cheap pulp that bills and solicitations arrive in. My first thought was that it came from a law office, and I tried to think who might be suing me. Probably Mr. One-Ball from Danny's botched booster pinch. But there was only a discreet return address on the outside—no name, and lawyers invariably listed the firm's name in bold fourteen-point copperplate. It gave them free advertising.

It took me a little time to place the address, and when I did I was half curious, half reluctant to see what the envelope held. I poised the letter opener over the flap and paused, like a surgeon taking a deep breath before making that first cut.

Inside I found a folded note—a single sheet of the same paper stock. Tucked into the fold, I found two tickets. I opened the page and read the delicate handwriting.

Nate,

I know what we agreed upon, but I needed to do something to express my gratitude, and Dusty told me that you were a fan. It's not much, but I hope it's not nothing. I hope you'll enjoy the show and that you'll think of me from time to time. I will you.

Audrey

The two tickets were for Count Basie's final L.A. performance, at the Shrine

Auditorium. Two VIP tickets.

"I'll be damned." I sat and stared at those tickets for a long time, fighting the urge to pick up the telephone and call her. In the end, good sense won out. It would only open a wound for both of us that was just starting to heal.

* * *

Dusty was skeptical. His idea of orchestra music tended toward Bob Wills and the Texas Playboys. I told him it wasn't going to kill him to expand his musical horizons. I pointed out that he now had Basie in the jukebox at the Buscadero, even though I knew he'd only done that to razz me. And I said that it was only fair that he come along, since I owed the tickets in part to his busybody ways.

He finally gave in, and after much debate, I was even able to convince him that since the Shrine was quite a bit swankier than our normal haunts, he should leave off the cowpoke duds for one night.

I wasn't expecting much, but he surprised me by showing up at my office the night of the show in a gray flannel suit complete with three-point silk handkerchief in the breast pocket and a chocolate brown fedora. I had no idea that he even owned any such garb. You think you know a guy... I told myself that maybe he'd strong-armed a banker on the way over, but I wasn't going to ask. The colorful, hand-painted tie he wore had a bronc rider pictured on it, but I had to allow him that. It went with the mustache.

For the occasion, he had also borrowed Pooter's Chrysler convertible, a chrome and butter-yellow beauty that was a good deal tonier than my beat-up Ford.

As though Audrey's gift and Dusty's sartorial switcheroo weren't surprises enough, fifteen minutes before we were going to leave for the Shrine, I looked out the window in time to see a long, blue Packard limousine make the turn off Hillhurst. It coasted into the gravel lot and pulled to a stop at the entrance to my building. I half-hoped, half-dreaded that I'd see Audrey step out, but Spencer emerged alone from the big car and walked into the building. As he did, I spotted Benjy, who was watching Monte for the evening, with his nose pressed to the glass of one of the diner's windows.

I listened as well as I could and still didn't hear him coming down the hall. The guy could have danced on a carton of eggs. In a minute, the office door opened softly, and Spencer came in with a clearing of his throat.

"Spencer, I'm surprised to see you," I said. "Everything okay at the Chase manor?"

"Good evening, Mr. Ross, Mr. Vanner. Yes, sir, the ladies are well, and both send you warmest regards."

"What brings you down into what passes for civilization?"

"Instructions from Miss Chase, sir. I am to drive you to the Shrine Auditorium." He gave Dusty's getup a curious eye. "I take it Mr. Vanner will be accompanying you?"

"That he will. He's never heard a tune that didn't have a banjo in it."

"Very good, sir." I knew that was as close to a laugh as I would ever get out of him. "Shall we be off?"

* * *

I would have declined the ride, but didn't want to offend Audrey's generosity or Spencer's sense of duty. We followed him down and even allowed him to open and close the door for us. As he eased us out onto Hillhurst and headed south, I noticed that not only had Audrey set us up with transport, but refreshments, too. A bottle of champagne rested in a big silver ice bucket, alongside two little silver dishes of caviar.

Since she'd gone to the trouble, I thought it would be ungracious of us to pass on the delectables. I uncorked and poured the champagne and handed Dusty a flute. When I passed him a silver dish with its tiny spoon, he sniffed at it and made a face.

"What the hell's that?" he said. "Smells like fish eggs."

"It's caviar," I said. "It's a delicacy."

He handed the dish back. "Whatever you call it, that ain't food, it's bait."

I ate my caviar and Dusty's too. By the time we passed by MacArthur Park, the champagne was half gone, and I was feeling pretty chipper.

* * *

The Shrine is a huge, terracotta colored affair that looks like a palace out of the Arabian Nights with its two big domed cupolas. The theater is massive, bigger than Radio City Music Hall, with over six thousand seats. With Count Basie doing a farewell show, I was guessing they'd all be filled.

The place was lit up like a movie premiere when we arrived. Cars lined the streets for a block around, and we were far from the only limousine in the parade. Spencer fell in line at the VIP entrance, and when our turn came, again insisted on opening our door.

We presented our tickets, and an usher showed us to our seats in a private orchestra box. Audrey had definitely pulled out all the stops.

The show, once it started, lived up to all the buildup and then some. Up to then, I'd only ever heard Basie's music on scratchy 78s and through tinny radio speakers. Hearing it live, with the musicians standing on stage smiling out at the crowd and clearly enjoying every minute as much as we were, I felt like I'd never heard it at all before.

Lester Young's tenor sax had never sounded as clean and bright. A live performance seemed to give extra energy to his free-floating style. Buck Clayton's trumpet cut like a knife. Jimmy Rushing's vocals rang from the mile-high ceiling, and you could feel his low notes vibrate in your chest. Whether the Count was playing simple rhythm licks or more complicated passages, he made it all look effortless and made the keyboard sing.

The band played a few of my favorites, and a few others I'd never heard before. I could see I'd been right about the crowd—looking out over the auditorium, I couldn't pick out an empty seat. But that audience of thousands sat as quiet as a church congregation through *Honeysuckle Rose, Georgianna, One o'Clock Jump, Red Wagon...* Until each final note, when the applause shook the walls like an artillery barrage.

I waited, hoping and anticipating, and in the last set was finally rewarded with the one-two, one-two piano intro and growling horns that led into *Blues in the Dark*. I hadn't thought that Rush could ever top his performance on the recording, but he proved me dead wrong.

* * *

After the concert, Spencer wrestled us through the throng of cars leaving the place, and in the light, late traffic, we were back at the office before Dusty and I had knocked off the rest of the bottle of champagne.

This time, it was Dusty who affronted Spencer by opening the limousine door. "I ain't the king of England, pardner," he told the chauffeur as we climbed out.

"Well," I asked Dusty as we stood enjoying the cool night air. "What did you think?"

"*Well*," he repeated in his Texas drawl. "I won't say you've made me a true believer, but I might put an extra record to two in the juke." With that, we said our goodnights, and he sped off into the night in Pooter's cushy carriage.

After some resistance, I managed to persuade Spencer to come up to the office and join me in a nightcap. I thought it was the least I could do for the guy.

I figured the stodgy Englishman might prefer Scotch, but I only had bourbon on hand, so bourbon is what I poured. If he minded, he was too polite to complain.

We drank a toast to Beth Chase's safe return, a second to Audrey's life returning to normal, and a third to Jimmy Singer's long—or preferably short—stay in prison. We talked a little while about life in the Chase household, though Spencer spoke with his usual reserve. He did let slip that after things settled down, Audrey had seemed "a tad bit blue" but that she appeared to be on the mend.

When conversation and my half bottle of bourbon ran out, we decided the time had come for each of us to be on his way. Spencer needed to get back to the estate, and I needed to reclaim my dog before Benjy stuffed him so full he wouldn't fit in the car.

I walked Spencer down to the limousine. He offered me a gloveless hand once more. "Should you ever have need of my services, Mr. Ross," he said, "I am at your disposal."

"Likewise, pal." He slid in behind the wheel, and as I prepared to close *his* door for a change, I had a thought. "You know, there is one thing you can do for me right now."

"Of course, sir."

"Tell me once and for all—is Spencer your first or last name? I've gotta know."

"May I ask, sir, why this is of importance to you?"

"It's the one remaining mystery in this whole screwy rat's nest of mysteries. The last question, and I hate unanswered questions."

He took a deep breath before he replied. "Spencer is my family name, sir. Although we are not, I should point out, the Spencers of Blenheim Palace."

"Thanks for the clarification." I didn't know Blenheim Palace from the Polar Ice Palace. "And what's your first name?"

"Really, sir." He stared straight out through the windshield. It was dark, but in the streetlight I thought I saw a little color rise in his cheek.

"Come on," I said. "Be a sport. Don't forget, I'm a professional secret keeper."

He stared some more. "It's Comberton, sir."

"Comberton?"

He nodded without looking at me. "Comberton Spencer." Then he turned to face me. "I trust that is sufficient to satisfy your inquisitive nature?"

"In spades, pal. And have no fear—neither wild horses, L.A. coppers, nor Aggie Underwood herself will ever drag that information from me."

"I'm grateful for your discretion, sir."

"Take care of yourself, Spencer."

"Good night, Mr. Ross."

He drove away, and I walked over to the diner to relieve Benjy of his charge.

* * *

As we drove home, I thought over what a strange week it had been. And this strange night seemed like the perfect capper. Dusty dressed like a citizen. A champagne and caviar limousine ride. Count Basie and *Blues in the Dark*. And Comberton Spencer.

I was grateful for Audrey's gift even though I saw it for what it was—a final goodbye. Anyway, I'd given her a parting gift of my own. Queenan had been curious to find the source of Griffin Glenn's five hundred a month, and I'd convinced him that since the guy was dead and we had his killer, it wasn't worth worrying about.

Thinking about Audrey and last farewells started to give me my own case of the blues.

"Don't worry, pal," I said as I reached over to stroke Monte between his ears. "They'll pass. They always do."

About the Author

J.R. Sanders is a native Kansan and longtime denizen of the L.A. suburbs. He's authored books on topics as diverse as Southern California apple farms and Old West lawmen killed in the line of duty. His debut novel *Stardust Trail*, a detective story set among the B-Western film productions of 1930s Hollywood, was a 2021 Spur Award Finalist (for Best Historical Novel), and Silver Falchion Award Finalist (for Best Investigator). *Dead-Bang Fall*, second novel in the Nate Ross series, was a 2022 Shamus Award winner (Best Original Paperback P.I. Novel). *Bring the Night*, the third Nate Ross novel, was a 2023 Shamus Awards Finalist (Best Original Paperback P.I. Novel).

J.R. lives in Southern California with his wife, Rose, and rescue dogs Ruby and Marlowe.

AUTHOR WEBSITE:

jrsanders.com

SOCIAL MEDIA HANDLES:

Facebook: facebook.com/jrsanderswest

Instagram: instagram.com/jrsanderswest
LinkTree: linktr.ee/jrsanders

Also by J.R. Sanders

The Nate Ross series:
   A Killing Way (Level Best Books, 2024)
   Bring the Night (Level Best Books, 2023)
   Dead-Bang Fall (Level Best Books, 2022)
   Stardust Trail (Level Best Books, 2020)

Some Gave All: Forgotten Old West Lawmen Who Died With Their Boots On (Moonlight Mesa Associates, 2013)